KONOSUBA: GOD'S BLESSING ON THIS WONDERFUL WORLD!

Runaway Goddess, Come Home!

16

NATSUME AKATSUKI

ILLUSTRATION BY
KURONE MISHIMA

YEN ON

NEW YORK

KONOSUBA: GOD'S BLESSING ON THIS WONDERFUL WORLD! 16

NATSUME AKATSUKI

Translation by Kevin Steinbach
Cover art by Kurone Mishima

KONO SUBARASHII SEKAI NI SHUKUFUKU WO!, Volume 16: DASSO MEGAMI, GO HOME!
©Natsume Akatsuki, Kurone Mishima 2019
First published in Japan in 2019 by KADOKAWA CORPORATION, Tokyo.
English translation rights arranged with KADOKAWA CORPORATION, Tokyo, through TUTTLE-MORI AGENCY, INC., Tokyo.

English translation © 2022 by Yen Press, LLC

Yen On
150 West 30th Street, 19th Floor
New York, NY 10001

Visit us at yenpress.com
facebook.com/yenpress
twitter.com/yenpress
yenpress.tumblr.com
instagram.com/yenpress

First Yen On Edition: March 2022

Yen On is an imprint of Yen Press, LLC.
The Yen On name and logo are trademarks of Yen Press, LLC.

Library of Congress Cataloging-in-Publication Data
Names: Akatsuki, Natsume, author. | Mishima, Kurone, 1991– illustrator. | Steinbach, Kevin, translator.
Title: Konosuba, God's blessing on this wonderful world! / Natsume Akatsuki ; illustration by Kurone Mishima ; translation by Kevin Steinbach.
Other titles: Kono subarashi sekai ni shukufuku wo. English
Description: First Yen On edition. | New York, NY : Yen On, 2017–
Identifiers: LCCN 2016052009 | ISBN 9780316553377 (v. 1 : paperback) |
ISBN 9780316468701 (v. 2 : paperback) | ISBN 9780316468732 (v. 3 : paperback) |
ISBN 9780316468763 (v. 4 : paperback) | ISBN 9780316468787 (v. 5 : paperback) |
ISBN 9780316468800 (v. 6 : paperback) | ISBN 9780316468824 (v. 7 : paperback) |
ISBN 9780316468855 (v. 8 : paperback) | ISBN 9781975385033 (v. 9 : paperback) |
ISBN 9781975332341 (v. 10 : paperback) | ISBN 9781975332365 (v. 11 : paperback) |
ISBN 9781975332389 (v. 12 : paperback) | ISBN 9781975332402 (v. 13 : paperback) |
ISBN 9781975332426 (v. 14 : paperback) | ISBN 9781975332440 (v. 15 : paperback) |
ISBN 9781975342050 (v. 16 : paperback)
Subjects: CYAC: Fantasy. | Future life—Fiction. | Adventure and adventurers—Fiction. |
BISAC: FICTION / Fantasy / General.
Classification: LCC PZ7.1.A38 Ko 2017 | DDC [Fic]—dc23
LC record available at https://lccn.loc.gov/2016052009

ISBNs: 978-1-9753-4205-0 (paperback)
978-1-9753-4204-3 (ebook)

10 9 8 7 6 5 4 3 2 1

WOR

Printed in the United States of America

KONOSUBA: GOD'S BLESSING ON THIS WONDERFUL WORLD!

16

Runaway Goddess, Come Home!

KONOSUBA: GOD'S BLESSING ON THIS WONDERFUL WORLD! 16

CONTENTS

Runaway Goddess, Come Home!

Please look for me.
—Aqua

Illustrations/Kurone Mishima
Design/Yuko Yaoya + Nanafushi Nakamura (Mushikago Graphics)

"I think my time may finally have come."

Kazuma

KONOSUBA: GOD'S BLESSING ON THIS WONDERFUL WORLD!

Runaway Goddess, Come Home!

Characters

Aqua

Job — **Arch-priest**

An untamable goddess of water. Specialty: party tricks.

Kazuma Satou

Job — **Adventurer**

Our NEET protagonist. His Luck is his only decent trait.

Darkness

Job — **Crusader**

A tanky knight with a major masochistic streak. Daughter of an influential noble house.

Megumin

Job — **Arch-wizard**

Genius of the Crimson Magic Clan. Not interested in anything except explosion magic.

Chomu-suke

Emperor Zel

Vanir

A major demon (age unknown). Helps out at Wiz's shop.

Wiz

Runs the magic-item shop in Axel. A Lich but also a pacifist.

A Search for This Runaway Goddess!

1

You'd think our self-proclaimed goddess would be wise enough to know better, but she wasn't: She'd run away from home. That might sound unbelievable, but it's true. Aqua left a note; then she hit the road.

As for the rest of us...

"I think you know why we've asked all you adventurers to come here. Rumor has it that the Demon King's forces are going to attack our town."

No, we didn't go after Aqua. We went to the Adventurers Guild. They'd summoned us at the worst possible time. I had half a mind to ditch them and go chase after Aqua, but I couldn't just abandon this town to fend for itself, could I?

At the Guild, the tables had been arranged in a circle so that Axel's adventurers could all see one another as they crammed in.

The meeting was supposed to serve as an impromptu task force to address the Demon King's plan to attack Axel. Under interrogation, Serena (currently in jail) had revealed that the attack plan would move forward even without her, its commander, and that there was no stopping it. Things didn't look good, and everyone was frowning at one another when a wizard woman raised her hand.

"Do we know when they're going to attack? Or how large their force is? If we knew when they were coming, maybe we could request a detachment of knights from the capital to reinforce us…"

There was some nodding at that, but the receptionist leading the discussion—I'm pretty sure her name was Luna—shook her head. "According to the general we captured, the original plan was to use enemy elements inside Axel so that only a small attacking force would be necessary. However, now that their commander has been captured, I think we can expect them to come in force to try to get her back."

I guess she *was* a general of the Demon King, after all; if she was alive, they would naturally want to rescue her.

Luna went on. "We don't know what their numbers are going to be, but we anticipate a difficult battle, since just about everyone in Axel is a novice adventurer. As for getting help from the capital… As it happens, the main force of the Demon King's army will be assaulting the capital at the same time as the attack on Axel…" She sighed, looking like she might burst into tears. "In other words, we have to act on the assumption that we won't be receiving reinforcements. If our nation's central government was to fall, it wouldn't matter if Axel survived. Every guild in every town has been informed of the planned attack, and the most capable adventurers and knights are streaming into the capital. We're going to have to protect Axel on our own."

A cloud settled over the gathered adventurers. This was the most serious threat we'd faced since Mobile Fortress Destroyer.

People started offering their thoughts in light of this better understanding of the situation. Maybe we could barricade the town gate and shut ourselves up inside, some said, or dig pit traps all around the periphery of the town, or arm the civilian populace, or create an emergency community watch… The ideas went on and on. Most of them weren't too terrible, actually, but none of them left the impression that it would actually be the key to saving Axel.

However, I didn't really notice any adventurers panicking, unlike when Destroyer attacked. All we were talking about was a difference in fighting strength. The opponents were just minions of the Demon King—our weapons would work on them just fine. This town might be full of low-level adventurers, but if they all banded together, things would work out somehow. That, at least, seemed to be the general, optimistic mood in the Guild.

.........*What should I do?* I kinda came here to ask everyone to help me track down Aqua. *Should I wait to go look for her until after Axel is saved?*

But Aqua had said that the Demon King's attack on the capital, when his castle would be all but empty, was our best chance. Which meant there was a possibility our wayward goddess would end up trying to storm the castle herself.

I was only Level 1—what good could I do if I stayed here? But with the crowd's momentum building, I kinda felt like it would take the wind out of everyone's sails if I said, *Hey, guys, I'm going away for a while—see ya.* It would probably sound like I was trying to weasel out of being part of the battle…

"Satou. Kazuma Satou. I don't see Lady Aqua anywhere. What's going on?"

The voice caught me by surprise as I stood there with my arms crossed, worrying. "…? …Oh, hey, Yamazaki."

"It's Mitsurugi! We're beyond a simple acquaintanceship by now; the least you could do is remember my name! H-hey, I know you do it on purpose, right? …W-well, forget it, just tell me what's going on with Lady Aqua. Isn't she with you today?"

It was Mitsurugi, the Sword Master with the enchanted blade and a pretty girl on either side of him.

"Aqua? She left a note and ran away from home. Anyway, what are you doing here? You've been all over the newspapers lately. I guess you've been killing it at the capital. Aren't you going to go help them out in their hour of need?" I asked him.

"When I heard Axel was in trouble, I came to help. This town is Lady Aqua's home base, after all. But…you say she ran away?" That got his attention. "Did you finally reach the end of her good graces? Lady Aqua is crucial. Where is she now?"

"Hell, I'd love to know. She wrote a note saying she was going to defeat the Demon King and left in the middle of the night. If she caught the last carriage before midnight, she's probably in Arcanletia by now. She thinks we've beaten enough generals of the Demon King that we might be able to break the barrier around the castle."

"Defeat the Demon King?!" You could hear Mitsurugi's shout all over the Guild. Everyone else fell silent. Mitsurugi had me by the lapels. "She said she was going to do that?! Lady Aqua, all by herself, left to defeat the Demon King?! Well, what in the world are you doing *here*?!"

"What do you want me to say? I only just learned Aqua was gone, and then they wanted everyone to come to the Guild, so here I am!"

When the rest of the adventurers heard what we were saying…

"Aqua left *all on her own*?! She's as good as dead!"

"And they *let her* go solo? There's reckless and then there's *reckless*! That late at night, there are probably undead all over the place!"

"Aqua can barely survive in ordinary everyday life. Even after all this time, she still gets lost in town occasionally. She'll never make it to the Demon King's castle!"

We had really stirred up a hornet's nest. Anyway, it was a little late for all the complaining.

"Calm down! Everyone, calm down, please! …Has anyone around here seen Aqua?" Luna asked. The Guild went quiet once again. People started offering bits and pieces of information but nothing that could definitively lead us to Aqua. What surprised me was how many people Aqua seemed to have become good friends with while I wasn't paying attention. Even adventurers I hardly talked to seemed to be on good terms with her.

…She really knows how to get along, doesn't she? No wonder she was so shocked when the puppeted adventurers had turned against her. Many of them had been her friends. And now she was making them all

worry! When I found her, I was gonna lecture her until she cried. That's what she got for upsetting so many people.

But to do that, first…!

Mitsurugi beat me to it. "I—I can't just stand here! I'm going after Lady Aqua! Kazuma Satou, what will *you* do?! You'll look for her, too, won't you? You'll come with me, yes?"

"B-but that leaves us in a bind!" Luna objected. "We need high-level adventurers like you to help with the defense of Axel, or at least of the capital…! I'll alert the guilds in the other towns and ask them to keep an eye out for Aqua…!"

Then we heard it: "Aw, let 'im go!" a certain gold-haired punk, already drunk first thing in the morning, shouted angrily. He was sitting in a chair, but he could barely stay upright, and he looked very upset. "Us here, we're more than enough to keep this town safe. Lissen, lady! There's lots of high-level adventurers here; you just don't know it. We don't need Harem Boy with his two girlfriends there to save us—we can do it ourselves!"

I wasn't sure if he sounded really cool or really stupid. Yunyun was sitting beside the punk—Dust, in case anyone was wondering—looking like she didn't know whether to stop this tirade or not. Then there was Keith and the other members of Dust's party, who definitely weren't going to stop him and, in fact, were openly enjoying the spectacle.

I was glad Yunyun had finally found some friends to hang out with at the Guild, but surely she could have picked better ones.

"Lots of high-level adventurers," though?

Luna, looking pained, gave voice to my question. "I'm sorry… *Do* we have that many adventurers above Level 20 here? I think most of our people range from Level 10 to Level 20. Typically, adventurers who surpass Level 20 leave this town and move to areas with more rewarding monsters. That custom means we would be lucky to have even a few people above Level 20 with us in Axel…"

So that was the story—everyone moved after they hit Level 20.

My party and I hadn't thought about it because we had a house here… and also because we seemed to struggle even fighting against small-fry enemies. But when you thought about it, we'd had a pretty high-level party…

Megumin had the highest level of all of us, and I didn't count because I'd gone back to Level 1, but other than that, our average had to be above 30. I didn't know how quickly the average adventurer normally leveled up, but with all the big bads we had faced over the past year, we'd advanced at a crazy-fast pace.

At that moment, a male adventurer got to his feet and said:

"Uh, I'm Level 32…"

"What?" Luna asked, shocked.

Another guy stood up. "Um…and I'm Level 38."

"*What?*"

One after another, the adventurers in the Guild stood and announced their levels. Every single one of them was over Level 30. A few had even passed 40.

Luna went around looking at their Adventurer's Cards as if she couldn't believe what was happening. "Wh-why in the world are you all still here when you have such high levels?! Surely it can't be very efficient to continue leveling up on the monsters around Axel?" She was as bewildered as she was amazed.

In response, one of the adventurers scratched his head, embarrassed. "Well, it's obvious, ain't it? We like this town."

Geez, that was the sort of awesome answer that could get a person's heart racing…

…and at that moment, I'm sorry to say, I realized. I knew why they were still here.

"Oh, e-everyone…! Let's do it! We can protect this town! With this many capable adventurers here, we can prevail! Let's give it everything we've got! If we all work together, we can save our home!"

While Luna and the other Guild employees were all but weeping tears of gratitude, I was busy noticing that all the high-level volunteers were men. And I recognized every single one of them.

Are you all *regulars at the succubus shop?*

2

There was an unusual excitement coursing through the Guild, but Mitsurugi ignored it and spread a map out on a table. "Here. This is the Demon King's castle," he said. He was pointing to a spot in the northwestern part of the map, marked with a symbol of a castle. Far to the south of the Demon King's hideout was another castle symbol representing the royal capital.

"As you can see, the quickest way to get to the Demon King's castle is to be teleported to the capital city and walk from there," he said. "Near the border between the two realms is the fortress you visited, Satou, along with a number of other small towns that have been turned into strongholds. We can restock provisions there." He traced the route to the castle with his finger.

Megumin, who was sitting beside me, spoke up. "Do you think Aqua, of all people, would take such a direct route? I'm sure she would think of a way to cause trouble or otherwise do some other weird thing... In any event, I'm confident she would get herself in over her head and not be able to take the direct path. Who knows? She might even still be near Axel, dawdling about getting ready to go."

Darkness and I were both nodding. We recognized an accurate description of Aqua's behavior when we heard it. Heck, knowing her, she might get tired—or scared—halfway and hang around for a while, hoping we'd come after her. In which case, she would take the longest, and safest, possible route. Maybe she'd hit every village along the way, letting her curiosity be her guide (and the cause of countless problems, no doubt).

I gazed at the map. "It's a longer route, but you can reach the castle via Arcanletia, too," I said.

Arcanletia: the "city of water." It was the home base of the Axis Church, and if you went northeast from there, you'd reach Crimson Magic Village. To the northwest, I could see a small road. It didn't look like much, but it led to the Demon King's castle.

I tried to think like Aqua. She had run away from home, and at first she'd be thrilled to be going on a little trip. Judging by the P.S. on her letter, though, she had already been questioning her decision. She was probably scared to go alone.

Notwithstanding all the high-level adventurers who had come out of the woodwork a few minutes before, this town was mostly populated by novices. If Aqua wanted to hire some help, she'd probably do it at a town somewhere along the way where she could hope to find people who were a little more powerful. And that meant…

"Knowing her, she probably made the bar to entry for her party way too high, just like back when we first got here."

When it had been just Aqua and me, she had put "only Advanced Classes need apply" on our want ads, and Megumin was the only person who ever inquired. If I wasn't mistaken, we had been looking for party members because we had our hands full with the simple quest of hunting five frogs.

"It does make one think of our humble beginnings," Megumin said. "As I recall, I had no money and hadn't eaten for several days, so was starving when I just happened to see the post soliciting party members…" She sounded really nostalgic.

"And when I saw Aqua and Megumin covered in frog slime, I knew this was the party for me," Darkness added. "The way Aqua was nearly driven to tears by that goop, and the way Megumin rode around paralyzed on your shoulders, Kazuma. Those two gave me the confidence that even I, as incompetent as I was, might be able to— Oh! Oh! Stop that, Megumin! I'm only telling the truth!"

I ignored Megumin, who had started pulling on Darkness's hair, and ran my finger over the map. "I think this is the route Aqua would take. She wouldn't go to the capital. She'd stick to a path she already knows. She'd hop on a carriage to Arcanletia, where she'd probably try to hire some other adventurers, but she'd set the bar too high, and no one would apply. So she wouldn't have a lot of options, but she'd still be too scared to go by herself, so instead she'd run crying to the Axis church in Arcanletia."

"Sounds right to me," Darkness said.

"Yes, I can easily imagine it," Megumin agreed.

"Wh-whoa, wait. What exactly do you all take Lady Aqua for?" Mitsurugi asked, the only one to object to our flawless prediction of Aqua's course of action. Come to think of it, he still didn't understand what kind of person Aqua was, did he?

"You don't have to like it, but I can almost guarantee that's what she's doing. We've known her a long time now. She's got a decent head start on us, but I'm sure she'll lose time getting into God knows what kind of trouble, so if we set out now, we can probably catch up with her."

Mitsurugi didn't look quite ready to believe me, but he nodded. "If you say so, you're probably right. Let's see, it's noon now… If we hurry, we can still catch one of today's tourist carriage departures. They don't go very fast, but they don't cost much, either. And if we move at a forced march after we arrive, we should be able to catch up with Lady Aqua. All right, we can do this."

Then he stood as if he was in a big hurry. Even Luna didn't try to stop him now. Things were what they were; she was evidently ready to let him go. Luna glanced at us and smiled slightly—she was probably worried about Aqua, too—and then announced to the adventurers in the Guild, "Okay, everyone, we're going to split up into groups! Those who already have parties, stick together! We'll assign you squad numbers and watches…"

The crowd started splitting into small groups and obediently lining up in front of Luna. Megumin, Darkness, and I, along with Mitsurugi and his two hangers-on, stood apart. Finally, as the adventuring parties each received a number…

…we saw Yunyun standing there, completely alone.

Shoot, that girl always was bad at finding a group or getting into a party.

Yunyun's eyes darted around in visible distress. Eventually, she spotted Dust and his party and went over to them, but she stood at an awkward distance, not quite with them, not quite apart from them, obviously hesitating.

Dust got on her case immediately.

"Hey, what do you think you're doing? You don't belong here."

That was pretty harsh, even in my book, but it reminded me of the first time I'd met him…and also reminded me that, yeah, this was pretty much what he was like (*sigh*). I'd thought maybe some of his rough edges had been smoothing out recently, but maybe it had just been my imagination.

"Uh, um… I'm s-sorry…" Yunyun bowed repeatedly and apologetically and backed away from Dust and his party.

Seriously, this was too much. I was about to give in and say something when:

"Where the hell do you think you're going? *That's* where you belong." Dust grabbed Yunyun, who was still sort of drifting away, and dragged her right over to us.

"…?" She looked at him, thoroughly confused.

"You've gotta be one of our top fighters in this town. If a genuine Crimson Magic Clan member and Magic Sword Boy here joined forces, you might even be able to give the Demon King a run for his money, yeah? When you see that troublemaking bastard, punch him in the face for me."

"Excuse me, but if Yunyun is a 'genuine' Crimson Magic Clan member, then would you please tell me what *I* am?!" Megumin exclaimed, but Yunyun just looked more confused than ever.

"Hey, I'm worried about these guys. If they bring home my girl Aqua, that's great, but I know them. They'll find some way to get into trouble. You're not some Arch-*whatever*; you're a real Arch-wizard, and you need to go with them… Aw, c'mon, you can use Teleport, right? If push really comes to shove, you can come back by yourself to help us."

Huh, this punk could talk a pretty good game when it really counted.

"I shall have you tell me to whom that remark about an Arch-*whatever* referred!" That was Megumin again, marching up to Dust.

"I understand. I'm going to go help Aqua! Because f-friends… friends help each other!" Yunyun was almost too embarrassed to get the words out, but she was smiling.

Luna, who'd been listening to the entire conversation, looked less than pleased to be losing someone who could use advanced magic, but she didn't say anything, probably because she didn't want to get in this punk's way.

"A Crimson Magic Clan member never backs down from a fight. So I accept your challenge. Come now, let us step outside!" Megumin had Dust by the lapels and was about to drag him away. Mitsurugi, meanwhile, smiled broadly and held out his hand to Yunyun.

"Looks like that settles it. All right…Yunyun, was it? Let's go together. It'll be nice to have an Arch-wizard along. Looks like you don't really have a party. Maybe when this journey is over, you can stay with me."

"Oh, um… That's all right…" Yunyun hesitantly took Mitsurugi's outstretched hand and shook it lightly, but she refused his invitation to join his party.

"………" He remained silent.

"H-hey, it's all right, Kyouya! You have *us*!"

"Yeah—yeah! Sure, having an Arch-wizard with us would be good for balance, but that girl is famous all over town for her wizardry! She's probably in high demand! So come on, chin up!"

Mitsurugi looked a little hurt, but at least he had his two friends to comfort him.

"Dust! Oh, Duuuuust!" I exclaimed. "Did you see her turn that hunk down flat? He tried to shake her hand like, *Hey, baby,* but she shot him down without a second thought!"

"Ha-ha-ha-ha, take that! Even Axel's loneliest wizard knows which friends are worth having!"

"Th-that's not what I—! I just thought that if I joined them, I would only cause them problems…! I'm t-t-telling you, I wasn't—! Kazuma, Dust, stop. You've got it all wrong!" Yunyun said, trying to stop Dust from whooping it up over Mitsurugi.

"G-geez! These guys suck! Kyouya, don't pay any attention to a couple of losers like them!"

"Hey, punk, get away from us! Go on, scram!"

Mitsurugi's little girlfriends scowled at us; meanwhile, Mitsurugi somehow got himself together. "O-okay, I think we'd better get going… So, pursuing Lady Aqua, we've got my two party members and myself, along with the four of you, including Satou. I think this could be an excellent opportunity, actually. With the Demon King's army attacking Axel and the capital simultaneously, there's probably only a few enemies at the castle itself. They've tricked themselves into thinking they can leave the castle undefended because of that barrier, but when Lady Aqua brings it down, we can storm the place. How about it? I think it'll work."

Wow. He sounded exactly like Aqua. And while I hated to spoil the mood, I had to say: "Sorry, but I'm not going after her. The whole reason I came to the Guild in the first place was so that I could post a quest to hire some high-level adventurers to do it for me. I mean, I'm only Level 1 right now."

"L-Level 1?" Mitsurugi said. "How did that happen? I mean, you were always weak, but…"

"Excuse me, I was always *what*? And I beat you *how* many times?"

Hey, if I had an overpowered enchanted sword like this guy did, I'd go after Aqua, too. But all I had were average stats (maybe even a bit below average, being the sheltered shut-in I was). I wasn't going on any journey.

"Forget about that. I can't believe you, Kazuma Satou! You've been with Lady Aqua for so long, yet you would leave her fate in the hands of someone else?! And you call yourself—! ...Hold on, there's something else you just said. *How many* times have you beaten me? The only time I ever lost to you was when you stole my enchanted sword from me... wasn't it?"

As Mitsurugi mumbled worriedly to himself, Megumin turned to me with an expression of distress. "Kazuma, is it true you are not going to get Aqua back? If it's your level you're concerned about, I expect it would rise at least a little during the trip..."

"I wanna go after her, but if there's one thing I know, it's that right now, one good punch from a goblin would probably kill me. You're high-level, Megumin, and Darkness is tough as nails, but I'd just slow you guys down."

Looking a little uneasy, Darkness said, "Don't worry. I'll protect you. So, Kazuma—"

"Look, we don't have Aqua with us this time. In other words, if I die in one of our little screwups again, I can't come back to life. Does our shared adventuring history inspire *any* confidence in me at all?!"

Megumin and Darkness both looked away.

"You know what I hate? Those heroines you see in anime and manga sometimes, who go running off on their own out of a misplaced sense of justice or sheer determination, all 'I *have* to do this...!' only to wind up captured by the enemy and causing trouble for everyone. I think if you're only going to get in the way, you should stay home and let the people with *real* power take care of things."

Let it be remembered that the whole issue here was that our failure of a goddess had gone running off on her own. But then there was the fact that her real objective was to defeat the Demon King and return to the heavenly realm. Even if we went after her and dragged her back, it wouldn't solve anything.

Mitsurugi looked like there was something he wanted to get off his chest. He sighed deeply and nodded. "All right, I see. Without any divine items or special abilities, at Level 1, you're just an ordinary high schooler. I won't ask you to go on a brutal journey in that state. But you won't object if I go after Lady Aqua and then work with her to defeat the Demon King?"

"Hey, if you think you can do it, be my guest, but I think you're throwing up a major death flag." Then again... "About what you said earlier... If Aqua and Yunyun both joined your party, you might actually have a shot at the Demon King. Balance-wise, it would be a pretty ideal group."

Mitsurugi looked surprised at my show of affirmation. Me, I didn't think this was just another enemy I could take out with sneaky tactics and sheer dumb luck. The Demon King was the last boss, and I figured I'd let someone with a proper cheat handle him.

In fact, things had been going a little *too* smoothly until now. I wasn't stupid enough to keep pushing ahead with no plan at all, relying on a convenient series of miraculous events. Now that I was Level 1 and completely powerless, it was time for me to take a step back and start going on adventures that suited my current abilities.

"Megumin, Darkness. In my situation, I would only get in your way, but both of you have fantastic fighting prowess. Go with Mitsurugi to look for Aqua. I'll stay here and hold down the fort." I knew that they, at least, would stand a chance against the Demon King, even if I wouldn't. The best thing for the entire world, then, would be to let them go with Mitsurugi, who was obviously eager to take on the Demon King.

Megumin, though, thought for a moment and then said, "No, I believe I will stay here. I know perfectly well that I am only useful in very specific situations. Without you to tell me what to do, Kazuma, I would probably use my magic on the first monster we saw, and then

I would be nothing but dead weight—no better than baggage. I think I will stay with you and wait for Aqua to get back."

"…In that case, I think I'd better stay here, too. It's a Crusader's duty to protect people, after all. I can probably be helpful in the defense of Axel. Besides…" Darkness looked at me as if there was something more she wanted to say.

"Wh-what?" I asked.

"No…," she said after a second. "It's nothing."

Geez, if she had something to say, she ought to just say it. Worse, now Megumin was looking at me like *she* wanted to say something, too.

Yeesh, you two. Get it together or I'll use Steal on you.

3

We saw Mitsurugi and Yunyun on their way, and then, without much to do, we went back to our mansion.

"We're home!" Megumin called as she opened the door, even though there was no one there to hear her.

Actually, there was someone: Chomusuke, drawn by Megumin's voice, came running to the front door.

"Oops, I cannot let you outside! There are dangerous vegetables growing in the garden. You must stay where I can see you until after the harvest." Megumin grabbed Chomusuke, who looked like she wanted to go outside and play, and held her in her arms.

Meanwhile, I thought about getting some weed killer and ruining those vegetables when the girls weren't looking.

Darkness came inside and looked around, seeming a bit down.

"…? What's going on? What's the matter?" I asked.

"O-oh, it's nothing, no big deal. It's just, whenever we all came back, Aqua would be the first to shout, *'We're hoooome!'*"

I guess she was lonely not hearing it.

Aqua had always been a bit of a whirlwind, but I had to admit, it felt weird not seeing her. Although part of that was because normally when I didn't see her, it meant she was off getting into trouble somewhere.

"Oh, Kazuma, did you see that we have a letter?" Megumin said, inspecting the little mailbox on our door. She passed me the letter. Just for a second, I thought maybe Aqua, feeling lost and alone, had sent a message begging for help, but when I saw who the letter was addressed to, I froze.

"Hot damn! It's from my little sister!"

"Don't say that! Say it's from Lady Iris!" Darkness exclaimed, but I completely ignored her and excitedly read the note…

> *Dear Kazuma,*
>
> *The leaves are falling, and the Snow Sprites have begun to show their chilly faces. Please forgive the suddenness of this letter. I'm writing to you about a matter of which I suspect you're already aware: The Demon King's army is planning to attack the capital in force.*
>
> *The attack is expected to be led by the last of the Demon King's generals, his own daughter. She's believed to be an exceptional commander; in the past, she even brought ruin to the famously combative Crimson Magic Village.*
>
> *I believe the battle between humanity and the Demon King's army is about to become very fierce indeed. I know those may sound like words of farewell, but there are many strong dark-haired, dark-eyed people like yourself, Elder Brother, here at the capital, so we should be all right. At the moment, not only members of the Crimson Magic Clan but elite fighters from all around the world are gathering here!*
>
> *I've heard that you recently lost your life while capturing the Demon King's general Serena. While it thrills me to know that you continue to fight as hard as you always have, I wish you wouldn't do anything too dangerous. It's my understanding*

that the Demon King plans to attack Axel as well, and I pray that you'll take care of yourself.

Your little sister will try to make you proud to be her big brother.

Yours,
Iris Stylish-Sword Belzerg

P.S. If I take out the Demon King's daughter, Elder Brother, will you tell me I did a good job?

"""" """"
....
I was silent as I finished reading.

…Hang on a sec. Were things really getting serious? I mean, sure, when I'd talked with Serena, she'd gone on and on about how humanity would never win or whatever. But what was this stuff about Iris making me proud to be her big brother and taking out the Demon King's daughter? It all sounded pretty dangerous, actually.

"Hey, Iris wouldn't really go into battle, would she? At times like this, they always have the princess run away to preserve the royal bloodline, right?" I said.

"Y-yeah, normally. But the Hero's blood flows especially strongly in Lady Iris's veins, even among members of the royal family. Our country is the main line of defense against the Demon King's army, and if it falls, humanity itself could be in real danger. Which means she might have to act as humanity's trump card…" Darkness's obvious discomfort was starting to make me worry, too.

"I'm sure she will be fine; after all, she is the flunky, grunt, and left hand of yours truly. I fully expect her to not only match the Demon King's daughter in battle but send her home crying as well."

Megumin sounded so nonchalant, but I felt a flash of rage. "I-if anyone important heard you talk about Iris that way, they'd have your head!" It was the same anger I'd felt when Serena had come to Axel and

I hadn't been able to do anything but watch her work. First Aqua, now Iris. People were getting themselves in trouble, and I was completely powerless to help. How pathetic was that?

But this was sort of how I had always been. I recognized this anger. It was the same way I'd felt watching my childhood friend—and first crush—riding away with some good-for-nothing older guy on his motorcycle, Back then, I'd tried to tell myself there was really nothing I could do about it, and that was when I had more or less stopped leaving my room.

But then I got a second chance in this world.

Dammit, at times like this, I really wished I had some sort of cheat ability. If only I had something, anything that could help me take on the Demon King, then *this* time—

Megumin and Darkness were whispering.

"He's holding his head and staggering around. What could it mean?"

"I think maybe he's overcome with sadness at the idea of a girl as young as Lady Iris going into battle... All right." Darkness coughed loudly. "Listen, Kazuma. If there's really nothing else we can do, how about we try to shake this off? Let's go back to where it all began...our mortal enemy."

Then she grinned.

4

I probably don't have to explain what "where it all began" and "our mortal enemy" meant.

We were in the field outside Axel.

"I keep telling you, I'm Level 1! If we let our guard down for even a second, that's it for me! Darkness! Darkneeeess! Hurry up and do something about this frog!"

A Giant Toad was hot on my heels.

"No, Darkness, you need to help *me*! I'm up to my neck already!

I've reached my record for 'most times swallowed,' and I am in trouble!" shouted Megumin, who had already used up her spell and was now neck-deep in a frog's gullet.

"Just try to slow it down—that's the only useful thing you can do right now!" I shouted. "If this frog gets me, we'll be stuck until Darkness learns how to hit the broad side of a barn!"

"You can only say that because you have relatively little experience being swallowed by frogs, Kazuma! Remember your instinctive fear, the primordial terror of being consumed that all animals have…!"

"You're the one who said being swallowed by a frog was nice and warm on a cold day!" I shot back.

Darkness was after the frog that was after me, holding her great sword and shouting, "Kazuma, I can't do anything about him when he's moving, so just stand still for one minute! It'll be fine—trust me!"

"How am I supposed to trust you right now?! …Oh, I've got it! Your Decoy skill! Why are you trying to attack him? Use Decoy and draw him off!"

"I've *been* using Decoy! But even frogs can learn and evolve! I'm wearing metal armor, and these guys hate metal armor, so I don't think it's working very well!"

Dammit, of all the times for her to come up short!

I grabbed the wire at my hip and thrust it at the frog behind me. "*Biiiind*!" Once I was sure my special wire had bound the creature up, I came to a halt, breathing hard. "Man, I really made the right choice not letting my emotions sweep me up into going after Aqua."

"H-hey, hold on! Decoy works fine on things that aren't frogs! Trust me next time!" Darkness stammered, but I ignored her; I went over and finished off the immobilized amphibian. Yeah, it was cheap. But that's life.

I said a little prayer for the creature I'd killed, then started working my wire free.

…Yes, *I started working my wire free.*

"…Huh?"

Something seemed very wrong. Wait…why could I use skills at all? I took out my Adventurer's Card and looked at it. Thanks to the frog, my Level had increased from 1 to 2. And…

"I got a skill point," I said, staring vacantly at the card.

Darkness, wondering what was going on, said, "What's the matter, Kazuma? Something wrong with your card?"

"Nah… I mean yeah, I guess. Heh…" I turned toward Darkness and smirked. "I think my time may finally have come."

And then I showed her the SKILLS section of my card.

"'My time may finally have come,' indeed! And, Darkness, how could you forget about me being swallowed by that frog? How can you still call yourself a Crusader whose duty is to protect her friends?!"

""I'm very sorry.""

Back home, Megumin was chewing us out (after she'd had a long bath). Overwhelmed by the magnitude of my discovery, I had completely forgotten about her. After I had proudly shown my card to Darkness, I turned to show it to Megumin, only to discover that she was fully submerged in the frog's mouth. We'd rushed to rescue her, but…

"The thing that makes me maddest of all is that you used Drain Touch to transfer MP to me! Normally, you'd just give me a piggyback ride. I'll bet you were afraid of getting covered in frog slime!"

"You read me like a book. B-but look, Megumin, now's not the time! I've made an amazing discovery! And it means I've got to go somewhere!" I said, trying to get the words out before Megumin succeeded in strangling me.

If this went well, it might be the start of my legend. "Wiz! I have to go to Wiz's shop! I'm not just going to sit at home and wait anymore! I've got something to take care of at Wiz's place, and then I'm going after that moron!"

That took Megumin and Darkness by surprise—and then they both smiled wider than I'd ever seen.

5

"Bwaaaa-ha-ha-ha-ha! Find her, indeed! What a truly troublesome goddess! A journey—glancing over her shoulder to see if anyone is following her even as she heads off to defeat the Demon King?! Bwa-ha-ha-ha-ha-ha!"

That was the delighted, cackling reaction I got when I showed the demon part-timer my discovery.

"Vanir, you're laughing too hard! Do you realize Lady Aqua went off on a journey by herself?! Oh, what shall we do?! Knowing her, I'm sure she'll get caught up in something terrible and end up crying...! What Lady Aqua said the other day, about sending me to the next life... It was about breaking the barrier around the castle, wasn't it?" Wiz was reading Aqua's letter over and over, torn between chastising Vanir and being in a complete tizzy.

I'd come to Wiz's Magical Item Shoppe to buy a certain something... "Vanir, give me all the level reset potions you have! I don't even care if you rip me off!"

Everyone except Vanir stared at me.

"K-Kazuma, what do you mean to do with those?" Darkness asked.

"Reset my level, obviously! By raising my level up and down, I can become one of those cheat protags!"

My discovery? Even when my level dropped back to 1, I didn't lose the skills I'd learned. And I retained all my leftover skill points, too. *And* just killing frogs was enough to raise my level, which resulted in more skill points each time. It was such an outrageous way to farm unlimited skill points that I couldn't believe no one had thought of it before.

I was practically bursting with excitement over my great idea, eager to tell everyone about it...

"I see, I see," said Vanir, looking at me intently. "You have some very interesting ideas, human. So you plan to lower your level and then raise it back up, repeatedly, as a way to accumulate skill points..." (I wished he would stop using his powers of foresight to get ahead of a guy and give away his plans.) "I must say, though, that one wouldn't normally go out of one's way to do that even if one had the means."

"They wouldn't? Why not? You can get unlimited skill points, right?"

Vanir snorted, which ticked me off.

"Most people don't need skill points *that* badly. Everyone is born with a certain number of them. I suppose in a broad sense, one might call it *talent*. I believe that damnable goddess acquired every skill with her starting points the moment she became an Arch-priest, yes?"

Come to think of it, in addition to knowing a bunch of party tricks, Aqua had said something about learning every single Arch-priest skill.

...Huh?

My starting skill points had been zero... Was that supposed to mean that I had no talent at all?

Vanir, ignoring my private depression (which he could no doubt see), continued. "We may consider that cheating goddess to be an outlier, but still. Take the members of the Crimson Magic Clan, for instance: They're born with the potential to be great wizards, and almost all of them know advanced magic. That's because as soon as they become Arch-wizards, they have enough skill points to acquire it. And if they don't, their friends help them gain experience through the method they call *farming* or by using items they call *skill-up potions*, until they are able to master the skill. Once you have advanced magic, of course, it's a trivial matter to raise your own level."

There was only one exception to the all-Crimson-Magic-Clan-members-know-advanced-magic rule, and she was standing next to me.

Okay, so maybe Megumin and Darkness had weird ideas about how to use their skill points, but they *did* have them; if they'd put their points into normal things, there wouldn't have been any problem.

"Okay, but everyone must want loads of skill points, right? If hunting a few frogs outside town can get you a level or three, why wouldn't the beginners here just do that every day and then pretty much start with all the skills in their class?"

"………Um, Kazuma…," Megumin said hesitantly.

"…?"

"You know it's not usually that easy to raise your level, right? Typically, under optimal conditions, it takes around one year to get to Level 10. And to reach Level 20, the level at which it's generally considered safe to leave Axel, takes upward of five years."

"Megumin can wipe out hordes of strong enemies with her Explosion, and I'm able to afford XP-packed food, so both of us advanced faster than the average adventurer," Darkness said. "But you, Kazuma…"

They couldn't quite bring themselves to say the rest, but then Vanir broke in merrily. "It's the way of this world: There's no one whose level goes up as easily as someone with no natural talent at all!"

""Oh!""

…As I began to fiddle with the nearby merchandise, Vanir said, "In any event, the only reason you can speak so nonchalantly of resetting your level is because you come from another world. When one's level goes down, one becomes weak. Those born and raised in this cruel land resist the idea of growing weaker even temporarily; every instinct as a living creature cries out against it. Only you, coming from a peaceful world, could accept the idea so readily. Besides, so long as they don't seek specialized skills such as explosion magic, most adventurers have all the abilities they need by the time they become veterans. Hardly anyone remains a member of the weakest class forever, as you have."

""……*Another world?!*""

Megumin and Darkness were still stuck earlier in the conversation. Come to think of it, I guess I'd only ever told them that I came from a faraway country.

"I don't understand. Kazuma, are you not a native inhabitant of this world?" Megumin asked.

"…I do seem to recall you saying once that you were from a faraway country…"

Stupid Vanir, bringing that up at a time like this.

"Listen, I'll tell you all about it some other time. Anyway, I get it: People from this world don't like resetting their level. But *I* don't mind, so sell me some level reset potions!"

"I'm sorry to say that I don't have any left. They're technically forbidden, you know. You're not even supposed to create them."

Huh?

"You've been leading me on, you bastard! I know you can 'see all,' so you knew what I wanted this entire time!"

"Bwa-ha-ha-ha! Yes, and what *I* wanted was to feast on your bad vibes! However, my dear boy, it's too early to give up yet. As thanks for this sumptuous feast of disappointment, let me offer you a bit of advice."

What a jerk. Just because Aqua wasn't here, he thought he could tease us to his heart's content!

"The important thing is, you want to raise your level, right? Among the status ailments in this world, one of the most reviled is called Level Drain. If you were to make strategic use of a monster who can employ this attack…"

"Y-yeah, I get it! Then I could raise and lower my level pretty much at will!"

I was thrilled to see a light at the end of the tunnel; Vanir nodded happily. "Mm, indeed. The caveat is that only a small number of exceptionally powerful undead creatures can use Level Drain. Normally one would never even encounter them, let alone manipulate them into using their abilities in specific ways. I'm quite pleased to inform you, however, that we have a friendly Lich—the very quintessence of powerful undead—right here!"

"Awesome! Unlike a certain goddess, you actually come through every once in a while!" (Vanir's lip curled at the comparison.)

"U-um," said Wiz. "Liches do have the Level Drain ability, but unfortunately, it's not possible to intentionally inflict a specific status ailment. It's one of several ailments that can occur randomly when a Lich attacks a hostile enemy. Others include Curse, Sleep, Magic Seal, and Panic. Critical ailments include Petrification and even Instant Death…"

"Huh, is that right? Sorry to hear that. Oh well, let's just pretend this conversation never happened…"

Megumin and Darkness grinned at each other to hear me give up so promptly on farming skill points (even if they did look a little exasperated about it).

Hey, even I value my life.

"Effort and exertion are right and proper for humans. Gaining too much power too easily invites karmic retribution. And power gained easily is almost always accompanied by significant drawbacks," Megumin said, and suddenly I found I couldn't help thinking of Aqua, whom I'd brought here as my "special item" when I was reincarnated. She'd caused me an awful lot of trouble, sure, but when I considered my own thought process—*If I bring along a goddess who can grant cheap powers, I'll be more powerful than anyone; it's like being told you have one wish and wishing for unlimited wishes*—I couldn't help feeling like I had gotten my just deserts.

I was feeling a little defeated—words like *karmic retribution* and *significant drawbacks* had hit me right in the heart—when Darkness said, "We're talking about attacking the Demon King's castle and defeating the king himself. I'm sure he'll be well protected. I think in this case, a frontal assault would be the only option. That means it's just like you said: Mitsurugi's party along with Yunyun and Aqua would be a pretty good combination. The whole reason the barrier around the castle is weak enough for Aqua to bring it down is because of your excellent work, no question. You've done your job, Kazuma. It's okay for you to take a breath now."

"She's right. Anyway, this is Aqua we're talking about. It's quite possible she's on her way home right now, too scared to go all the way. We should be waiting for her when she gets back, with a properly prepared lecture, of course."

It wasn't like Darkness and Megumin to be so gentle on me.

………No, the truth was, even I understood. Deep down, I wanted to take Megumin and Darkness and go after Aqua and make her dream of defeating the Demon King come true.

Then there was my one brag-worthy quality—my Luck stat, which was so absurdly high, it was practically a cheat ability.

I looked at the girls who were trying to console me with smiles of defeat, and I made my decision.

"Hey, Wiz. Can I ask what destinations you have registered with Teleport?"

The spell might have been called Teleport, but it wouldn't send you just anywhere. You had to have the destination registered first, and you could register only up to three places.

Wiz looked confused, but she said, "One of my destinations is Axel's town gate. I overwrote the second one and made it Crimson Magic Village, for business purposes."

"Wiz, you should immediately overwrite Crimson Magic Village with somewhere else." Vanir was frowning. What did he have against her going there?

"And lastly, in order to be able to gather magical ingredients, I've registered the entrance of what's said to be the deepest dungeon on the continent…"

"That's it!" I exclaimed. I remembered: Back in the battle with Mobile Fortress Destroyer, Wiz had been sent to that dungeon with Random Teleport by a rock called Coronatite, and she said she'd registered it as one of her Teleport destinations just for good measure. A dungeon like that ought to be overflowing with experience points—er, I mean, powerful monsters.

I turned to Wiz and bowed my head. "Wiz, train me in that dungeon. And then, after my level goes up, use Level Drain on me, right there in the depths."

"What?!" Wiz cried, and Megumin and Darkness looked almost as amazed as she did.

"Kazuma, were you even listening?! A Lich's status-ailment attack is terrible! You could conceivably be petrified or even killed on the spot, and for someone as weak as you, the HP-sapping Curse could be fatal as well!"

"You're always so interested in covering your own neck, and then sometimes you say the craziest things! Aqua's not here right now. If you die..."

Yeesh, didn't they ever shut up? "Ugh, pipe down, you two!" I snapped, now totally in the grip of my own brilliant idea. "I want you to hit the town and find every adventurer you can who has any useful skills! Tell them that as soon as I get back from the dungeon, I want them to teach me their abilities!"

There was Megumin, who'd sworn she would defeat the Demon King and show everyone up ever since the other members of her village had discovered she could only use Explosion and made fun of her, calling her a *"joke wizard"* and a *"spare mage."*

There was Darkness, who obviously wanted nothing more than to go after Aqua, but she held herself back instead and said she would watch the house.

And then there was Aqua herself, terrified to be out all alone but doing it anyway so that she wouldn't drag the rest of us into trouble with her.

Curse them all.

I mean, curse them all!

Normally they couldn't *stop* themselves from causing problems. So why did they have to pick the weirdest times to turn sensitive and thoughtful?! If they were capable of this level of human decency, I wish they would have shown it all along!

"I know people talk about me like I'm a good-for-nothing, like I'm a devil! But even I'm not such a loser that I would leave something like this completely in the hands of other people! So a Lich can inflict Level Drain, Curse, Sleep, Magic Seal, Panic, Petrification, and Instant Death, right?! Okay, so let's pretend that Curse, Petrification, and Instant Death are my losing hands. You two have known me long enough that you ought to know…with my Luck, I only pick winners. So come on, get going! Get out of here!!"

I did my best Aqua impression as I shooed them away, even making her little *shoo, shoo!* noises.

"A-are you insane, Kazuma…? At the very least, you should come back to Axel and have a priest cast Bless on you before you get your level drained… Something, anything…!"

"H-hold on, Kazuma, wouldn't it be best to have me along to shield you from the monsters, then…?!"

The girls were trying to object, but I all but shoved them out of the shop. Then I turned back to Wiz. "That's the plan. Sorry to impose, but do you think you could toughen me up? I know it's a lot to ask a former general of the Demon King to help me with this, knowing my objective is to bring down the king himself, but…"

"I-it's all right; I want Lady Aqua back as much as you do… But I can't guarantee I'll be able to protect you all by myself. It's a large dungeon. We could get lost, and there are dangerous traps… And above all, there's always the chance that my skill could kill…you… Oh! That's it!" Wiz had looked awfully down on the idea, but now she clapped her hands. "Vanir! With your ability to see everything, you would know whether I was going to inflict a critical ailment on Kazuma before I did it, wouldn't you?! A-and! And! You would be able to tell the best way through the dungeon and foresee any traps!"

"Absolutely not." With those two words, Vanir shot down Wiz's brilliant suggestion. And then he started laughing. "Bwa-ha-ha-ha! Yes, it was to obtain these bad vibes that I gave the kid such kind and helpful advice! Oh, delectable! The negative emotions the two of you are generating are positively exquisite!"

I was starting to hope I would get the chance to destroy this demon sometime.

"I don't particularly care what happens to the Demon King, but I don't see why I, a demon, should be obliged to help save a goddess! Bwaaaa-ha-ha-ha-ha-ha! Yes, excellent! Good fortune will come of that goddess getting lost on the road, munching on some weeds somewhere, and dropping dead! Well, it hardly matters. Someone like her will never, ever make it to the castle alone! Bwaaaaa-ha-ha-ha-ha-ha!"

"Vanir! Surely now of all times, you could see fit to help her. And if not, I have a thing or two to say about it myself!" Wiz said, suddenly deadly serious.

Vanir acted a bit taken aback. "Oh-ho? Then speak, if you believe you can threaten the great—"

"I have some stock here that I got in secretly, without letting you know. There turned out not to be very much of it, so I was thinking of returning it, but now I don't think I w— Oh! Stop, that's an important item that I don't have any intention of returning! Please stop trying to take it!"

I turned to Vanir and Wiz, who were struggling over some merchandise, and said, "Y'know, Vanir, I think I owe you a favor. If I get back from that dungeon safely, I promise I'll finally make good on it."

I dropped the words into their argument like a pebble into a pond.

"...? A favor?" Vanir, keeping one hand on Wiz's head to prevent her from grabbing the merchandise back, looked at me, perplexed.

"When Aqua had chased me out of our mansion, you helped me sneak back in in the middle of the night. I promised you I'd buy whatever overpriced crap Wiz stocked at the store, right?"

"Oh yes, that did happen… Wiz, I am going to sell off this junk you've acquired at a stroke! So—grrr, let go already! There's nothing important in any of this; I declare it all to be complete junk! And I'm going to sell the whole lot of it off!"

"No, wait, that's not junk! It's a rosary that's supposed to bring a wonderful encounter to anyone who possesses it…!"

They weren't done arguing, but I said:

"Sorry, but that's not what I plan to buy. I already know what I want. And I'm sure Vanir will be thrilled to have me take it off his hands…"

Midnight. I stood before the sleeping Emperor Zel, saying good-bye.

"I know you understand, Emperor Zel. If anything happens to me, it'll be up to you to save the world, all right?"

He was sleeping soundly inside his chicken coop, and despite having a goddess standing right in front of him, he showed no sign of waking up. I always knew he was something special. They say nothing sleeps as much as a long-lived dragon, and he kept right on snoozing even when bathed in the glory of a genuine goddess. I could only imagine how bright his future would be.

"Now listen, Emperor Zel. Even if they do terrible things to me, you mustn't destroy the world for the sake of revenge, okay? Your mommy wouldn't want that."

I had to make sure I emphasized that point to Emperor Zel; he loved me so much.

Emperor Zel continued sleeping, wholly unbothered by the fact that he was doing it in a demon's leftover skin. He showed no fear of either goddesses or demons. He truly deserved to become the emperor of dragons.

His fiery red comb, his golden beak, his pure-white feathers. I was just patting his soft wings in a gesture of farewell when I sensed something on my feet.

"Hello there, pitch-black magical beast. I know you usually get the better of me, but I have Emperor Zel with me now, so don't try anything funny, okay? If I even think you're going to attack me, I'll wake him up, and he'll wipe the floor with you."

Curled up at my feet for some reason was my mortal enemy, the mysterious magical beast Chomusuke. She didn't seem to think very highly of me. She never hesitated to steal my food or my snacks, and I wished she would knock it off.

"H-hey, what's going on? You seem awfully friendly today." Chomusuke was pressing her head into my hand silently, as if commanding me to pet her. Normally, she hardly let me touch her. That's how cats are, I guess. So selfish!

Huh, and she was actually pretty soft and fluffy. Sheesh!

"Could you be trying to stop me from going to defeat the Demon King? Don't be silly. If you think I'll put off leaving just because I got to pet a fluffy kitty, you're wrong. But…well, I *might* see fit to wait until tomorrow if I could pet your belly."

I'd tried my best to negotiate, but I guess Chomusuke wasn't willing to go that far, because when I reached out to rub her belly, she responded by baring her claws at me.

"You'll get divine punishment if you scratch the soft, supple skin of a goddess. I sense an inhuman aura from you sometimes; I wonder what that's about. You're a cat, and yet, you always smell nice. Are you hoping to become the goddess of soap? You can't be the goddess of the bath, you know; I won't allow another water-aspect goddess to move in on my turf."

Chomusuke started gnawing on my feather mantle as if to say she hadn't even been thinking about it. That was a divine garment, and I wished she would stop getting drool on it.

Suddenly, Chomusuke looked into empty space.

"Oh, did you come to see me off, too?"

Standing there was Anna, the ghost who haunted our mansion.

Normally, she put her heart and soul into teasing me, but she seemed to be in a different mood today.

"Why do you look so serious? Have you decided you're ready to move on?"

I'd chosen not to purify her because she'd said she would go on to heaven of her own accord when she'd heard enough of my adventuring stories, but…

"You're not even close to being tired of them yet? I see. Well, best for you to stick around, then, so you can pass on to the next life with no attachments to this one. But don't let Eris find you, okay? She can be awfully hardheaded—she's not flexible like I am."

Anna nodded at my warning.

"……Hey, don't say things like that. Isn't that what they call a death flag?"

She'd asked me for my best story, one last tale in case I didn't come home, so she would have something to remember me by.

I sat down on the lawn, and Chomusuke did something else unusual: She sat on my knees. "Gosh, I can't have you two acting like you're getting ready for a drawn-out battle. Anyway, I'm going to miss the last carriage…"

Chomusuke yawned as if she didn't even hear my objections. I wondered what was going on with her and Anna. Didn't they even know they were interfering with my attempt to defeat the Demon King?

But, well…

"Okay, okay. I'll tell you one of my favorite stories. It's from the time when I was working hard to guide deceased souls to the next life in the heavenly realm. One day, there was this NEET in a tracksuit who died in the silliest way possible…"

After all, how could I turn down a request from the ghost girl I'd known so long?

1

—Floor 1—

"Bwa-ha-ha! Bwa-ha-ha-ha-ha! Get lost, goblins! Go home! Or do you all want to become experience points for our customer? We have no interest in low-yield mobs like yourselves! Come now, make way!"

Vanir: Duke of Hell, former general of the Demon King, major demon. Normally, he could have passed for a last boss himself, but at the moment, he was walking ahead of us, scattering a crowd of goblins. As befitted a Duke of Hell, he looked noble and terrifying…

…Not. He was wearing beach shorts, sandals, and an open white shirt with nothing else underneath. Very "cool."

I questioned delving into a dungeon in an outfit like that, but I wasn't going to waste any energy worrying about this guy. The weirdest thing about it was that while everything else he was wearing was so loose and laid-back, he still had that mask right on his face. You'd think it would get in the way.

"I never dreamed the day would come when I would get to go on an adventure with you and Vanir, Kazuma! Today, I won't just be the worthless shopkeeper Vanir is always yelling at! I'll show you what I could do back when I was a great, famous mage!"

Wiz, behind me, sounded like she was having a great time. We were hitting the dungeon, with Vanir in front, Wiz in back, and me in the middle for safety. Today, Wiz didn't seem anything like her usual shop-keeping self, constantly panicked and failing at everything. She actually seemed like someone you could rely on.

But I had to ask…

"Vanir's one thing, but don't you need any weapons or armor, Wiz?" She'd come along still wearing her apron from the shop, and she looked almost as out of place as Vanir did.

He was practically dressed for the beach and carrying a cloth bundle over his shoulder; Wiz had an apron. I was the only one wearing real armor. I'm sure anyone who saw us would have wondered what the heck we were doing.

"It's okay! Liches can only be injured by magically enchanted weapons, attacks from monsters with powerful magic, or by actual magic attacks! I may not look like much, but I am a King of the Undead! In fact, this is the dungeon where I first met Vanir. Ohhh, I'm so excited!"

Wiz was raring to go, and I couldn't help feeling that I could really count on her. At the same time, I was starting to regret asking these two for help.

—Floor 5—

"Perfect! Flawless! I'm in top form today! Bwa-ha-ha-ha-ha! How insolent of a mere ogre to think it could oppose me! I needn't even resort to magic. I'll take care of him with my bare hands!"

"You certainly seem to be enjoying yourself, Vanir! But remember, you have to let Kazuma get the last hit or he won't earn the experience points…"

Vanir had gotten into a wrestling match with an ogre that stood at least ten feet tall; meanwhile, beside him, Wiz touched another group of ogres one by one. Some of them collapsed, frothing at the mouth; others fell unconscious and stopped moving. Those would be the Curse and Sleep status ailments, I assumed.

My job was to finish off the incapacitated monsters. I'd like to say it was a nice, simple way to gain experience points, but even I had some objection to murdering enemies who couldn't fight back.

I have to say, though, Wiz and Vanir lived up to what you'd expect from a couple of former generals of the Demon King. It was like they had invincibility mode turned on, like a whole horde of ogres meant nothing to them.

The dungeon Wiz had teleported us to was supposed to be the biggest and deepest around, and the width of the hallways and the height of the ceilings sure made it look like a dragon could walk around in here no problem.

We'd been down here for hours. My level, which had gone back to 1 in the fight with Serena, had shot past 10 and was quickly approaching 20.

I went over to an ogre Vanir had reduced to tears using Submission and stabbed it to death with my sword. "I think this last ogre should... Yes! Level 20! I'm flying through the levels, thanks to you two," I told them. I pulled my sword out of the body and put my hands together in a gesture of prayer for the deceased ogre.

I was raising my level pretty much the way you would in a video game, but to be honest, I felt a little weird about it. Maybe it was killing sentient, humanoid monsters that gave me the chills. But this was all so I could get stronger, so sorry, guys.

I was still praying as Vanir turned toward me with an unusually concerned look. "Hmm, so your level has gone up that much already... I thought you had no capabilities whatsoever as an adventurer, but that's quite a pace. Hmm... How do I put this...? One could say that the ability to gain levels quickly is its own kind of talent..."

"You're the last person I want pity from. At least cackle at me..."

While Vanir sympathized, Wiz reached out hesitantly toward me. "A-all right, here I go, okay? Vanir, is this going to be all right...?"

"Yes, no problem. I foresee a healthy, happy future for our dear customer."

I let out a breath of relief when Wiz had safely drained me back down to Level 1.

"It really worked. Phew!" Vanir said.

""Huh?"" Wiz and I chorused, goggling at him. What did he just say? I thought he knew the outcome…!

"Bwa-ha-ha-ha-ha! Were you worried? Fear not—I guarantee your safety at least until you're able to make the purchase you promised… Ooh, what fine bad vibes, absolutely delicious!"

Oh yeah. I'd almost forgotten who I was dealing with.

—Floor 10—

"H-hey, Vanir… Just how deep is this dungeon? I feel like we've been walking forever. I've got no idea how much time has passed. And I didn't bring any snacks with me…"

We had Vanir the All-Seeing Demon, Wiz the undead, and me with my Second Sight skill. We could all see in the dark, so we went through the dungeon without any kind of light. Even though I could see what was around me, I couldn't see *where we were going*, and that made me uncomfortable. Like I said, I had no sense of time down here, but it felt like we'd been in this dungeon for quite a while.

"My expectation is that the twentieth floor is the lowest in this dungeon. We've been down here for roughly half a day. And if you need food, I have plenty, so don't worry." He patted the bundle on his back. "Normally, one would explore a dungeon of this size in small increments, working one's way through it over the course of months. We've come this far this quickly only because I am able to discern the path and see all the traps. If you understand that, then feel free to make not only your intended purchase but others as well. Still… This is quite an impressive dungeon. Maybe once we make it to the bottom floor and defeat the dungeon master, I'll take control of the place for myself."

"N-no, Vanir, don't do that! *I'm* going to build your dungeon! And I still need your help at the shop!"

So we traipsed along, Vanir and Wiz so unconcerned that they were openly bantering. The smack of Vanir's sandals against the floor sounded weirdly out of place; it was almost enough to make me forget that I was down in a dangerous dungeon.

"Hey, what's with the outfit anyway? I promised myself I wouldn't ask, but I've just *got* to know…"

"Hmm? This outfit? It belonged to the deceased husband of a fine woman I know; she begged me to wear it. I was mucking out the neighborhood's roadside gutters in my suit when she suggested that this would be much easier to move in. What do you think? How do I look?" He showed off his Bermuda-shorts-and-shirt ensemble.

Frankly, it made him look like an old fogey on his way to the convenience store, but then there was the mask…

"You look like a rare monster that could only be found in a place like this," I said. If any adventurers spotted Vanir at that moment, they probably would have chased him down, thinking he was a unique monster.

"Hmm, so I look like a rare monster, do I? I'll have to express my gratitude to the woman who gave me these clothes." Apparently, demons considered it a compliment to be compared to a rare monster.

"You look even more at home in this dungeon than I do, Vanir," Wiz said. "Even after I lived *there* for so long…" She looked a little depressed.

Then, though, we heard voices from up ahead. My Sense Foe skill was tingling. There was a powerful enemy nearby.

"Look, there's a Cerberus down here! Its pelt always retains its warmth, making it a highly prized material in winter! Wiz, don't let it get away! If you catch it, I'll let you eat meat for a week!"

"I'm sorry, Cerberus! I want to eat protein sometimes! I love dogs, but… I'm sorry! I'm sor— Oh! Don't run away!"

—Floor 13—

"Grraaahhhh!"

"Bwa-ha-ha-ha-ha-ha! You fool! To think that a mere lizard could stand against me! Now, at last, we shall see who is stronger, dragons or demo— H-hey, Wiz, watch out! It's going to use its breath weapon! I'm trying to hold it down here, but I'm going to get fried!"

"V-Vanir, I told you, it might be a lesser member of the species, but it's still a dragon! They have powerful magic, and even I'll feel it if I get too close and it bites me!"

"I don't think this is the time, Wiz! Vanir... Vanir's going to get eaten!"

I was face-to-face with a real dragon for the first time in a long while. Wiz claimed this was a lesser dragon, but as far as its size was concerned, it still easily surpassed some storehouses. It looked like if it wanted a steak, it could probably just eat the whole cow!

"Argh, it ate my hand! There's nothing in this dungeon from which to reconstitute a body for myself. If it keeps eating, I'm going to disappear! Fine, we have no choice... Dragon scales sell for an exceptionally high price, and they yield a great deal of experience, but we have to give up on this creature! Wiz, finish it off with magic!"

"All right! Here I go! *Cursed Lightning!*"

Vanir was somehow managing to keep the dragon at bay despite the fact that it was chewing on one of his arms; from behind him, Wiz launched an electric attack. The dungeon darkness was obliterated by a flash of blinding light. The blue-white streaks perforated the dragon's body and continued to crackle with powerful sparks for a moment after.

As the sparks faded and the darkness returned, the dragon, now with a hole in its belly, fell to the ground with a huge *thump*.

There you had it: When a Lich got serious, she could take down a dragon in a single hit.

"Holy crap... So Liches are even stronger than dragons *and* demons?"

"...?!"

"Heh-heh, they don't call us the Kings of the Undead for noth— Wh-what are you doing, Vanir? Stop that! Keep your half-chewed arm away from me...!"

Vanir was giving Wiz a hard time; maybe he was feeling a little mean after seeing her so easily dispatch the dragon he'd been struggling with. As for me, finally free of the terror of a powerful enemy, I slumped to the ground.

"I'm almost Level 25 now. My level's shooting up after every battle, but even at this rate, I'm starting to wonder if this is as far as we should go. Even Vanir's getting a little winded…"

After Wiz had reset my level the first time, I'd hit 25 again super quickly. It was going so quickly that I was starting to wonder why I'd spent that year and change adventuring. Everything we'd beaten down here was a big enough monster that it would have wiped the floor with my usual party and me.

How long had it been since we'd come in here? The last time I'd asked, it had been half a day, so it was probably the middle of the night by now.

"What was that?" Vanir said, having picked up on my whining. "The only reason I'm 'a little winded' is because I'm working under the constraint of trying not to hurt the creatures too much and to render them powerless while keeping them alive. If I was allowed to simply annihilate them, I could easily walk down to the lowest level on my own!" He never did stop menacing Wiz with his arm as he spoke. Frankly, it was pretty gross to watch, so I wished he would hurry up and reattach his limb.

"But Kazuma is right—at this rate, we are going to struggle… Maybe this would help," Wiz said. Then she walked over to the dragon's corpse. "*Cursed Necromancy!*" she shouted at it.

It was then that I realized I had not been giving this Lich general of the Demon King nearly enough credit. The "penniless proprietor" of the starting town, still wearing her apron, had—

"Now then, let's turn a few more dragon-class monsters into undead… Since we're here and all, we might as well make a push for the lowest level of the dungeon." She put a hand on the head of her newly risen zombie dragon as if she was going to take it for a walk. Then she whispered to it that if they made it to the bottom, she would set the creature free. She sounded downright apologetic.

"Wiz, my opinion of you has gone way, way up since coming to this dungeon. You really were an incredible mage, weren't you?"

"O-oh, you think so? But I s-still have a long way to go…!" She almost sounded embarrassed. "Anyway, let's get started! Come on!"

I stayed slumped on the ground. "I'm sorry, but could we rest for a few minutes? I'm really tired. I know we got all the way here without stopping, but the moment I caught my breath and the nerves wore off, I realized how exhausted I am…"

Vanir sat down beside me and spread his cloth bundle on the floor. I'd assumed it was full of supplies for tackling the dungeon, but it turned out to be packed with potions, magical items, and daily necessities.

"Now, my good lad! I have here fatigue-relief potions, foodstuffs, water, medicine, and an Instant Barrier, among many, many other things." Leave it to an all-seeing demon to anticipate your every need. "Today, our dungeon branch is offering a special price! Only five times what these items cost in town! How about it, O valued customer?"

Leave it to an all-seeing demon to know when he's got you cornered.

…What a jerk.

2

How in the world did we get ourselves into this pickle?

"Oh no! It's coming after us! Stella! Stella!! Don't you have any more of those scrolls with Flash?! We need to blind them again!" Gil shouted. He was talking to me.

"I'm afraid not! The last one I used was… Well, it was the last one!" I was half shouting and half crying.

"We finally get a little treasure, and now we're done for?!" Gayne, the last member of our party and the one carrying the sack full of loot, wailed.

I kept running. I could feel the prickling in my nose, the tears starting to run from my eyes, but I couldn't do anything about them. I had only a small lantern to cut through the darkness of the hallway. Oh, how I regretted what we had done just a few minutes before! It was too soon for us to be down on the thirteenth floor of this dungeon.

We'd made it to the twelfth floor by doing a little exploration and mapping each day, carefully learning about the monsters and their habitats. We'd been at it for more than six months.

When we got to the twelfth floor, we'd found we had no trouble at all with the enemies there, and that had caused us to let down our guard. We'd been wrong, wrong to let our success go to our heads after so much careful work...!

It was believed that no one had ever completed this dungeon, and conventional wisdom had it that your level should be at least three times that of the floor you were exploring. It was a good guideline. And it meant that the thirteenth floor, which we were currently on, demanded at least Level 39.

Our average level...wasn't quite there.

There was only darkness behind me, but I could feel the monster breathing down my neck. "I don't want to die... I don't want to die...!" wept my little sister, who was running right behind me. The staircase to the twelfth floor was ahead. If we could just reach it, we could get away from the monsters pursuing us.

Monsters that inhabited dungeons weren't like those that occurred naturally on the surface. Dungeon denizens were typically summoned by someone or something, and they absorbed and were energized by the mana with which the summoner had imbued the dungeon. Unlike surface monsters, summoned creatures couldn't continue to exist without mana.

Some people claimed mana was the atmosphere of Hell, while others said it was MP in gaseous form, but whatever it was, it emanated from the innermost room in the deepest depths of the dungeon. And of course, the deeper you got—the closer to the Dungeon Master's chamber—the denser the mana became. Stronger monsters required denser concentrations of mana, but by contrast, weaker ones couldn't survive where there was too much of the stuff. So…

"We're almost to the stairs to the twelfth level! If we can just get up where there's less mana, these guys won't be able to follow us, no matter how persistent they are! We'll save ourselves if we can just get up there!" Gil sounded like he was trying to convince himself as much as the rest of us.

When those monsters ambushed us, our magical item that produces a temporary barrier—the most important thing to have when exploring a dungeon—broke. As if that wasn't bad enough, so did the bag with our provisions in it. In other words, we would be unable to rest anywhere in the dungeon. Unable to recover our MP. Even if we got away from these monsters, our chances of surviving to make it back to the surface weren't good.

But any chance was better than being murdered by those disgusting creatures…! We just had to get to the stairway, and then, unwilling to follow us up into the thinner mana of the floor above, the monsters would—

"Argh!" Gayne cried from the back of our formation, snapping me out of my reverie.

I looked toward the sound to see all our loot spilling out of his sack. I almost wanted to shout at him to ask what he thought he was doing, but *he* wasn't doing it. Instead, something with a shape almost impossible to describe had raked its claws across his back.

Realizing that Gayne wouldn't be able to run away now, everyone stopped. In the pitch blackness, we heard a sound: *shloop, shloop*. Something was coming toward us.

The monster moved with astonishing speed for something that crawled on the ground. It was just about to creep into our lantern light…

"So it's come to this! All right, Stella, no choice! Get your magic ready to go! Drop a spell on it, and while it's stunned, I'll—"

Over Gil's voice, I could hear *p-tap, p-tap*, like footsteps, this time from in front of us. Gil dropped whatever he had been about to say. He was overcome with a look of despair, and the other two made similar expressions and murmured that it was all over.

O gods, O gods... Please, at least let the monster in front of us be one that doesn't toy with its victims...!

"Welcome, welcome! You've found Wiz's Magical Item Shoppe— Dungeon Branch!"

....

""""Huh?!"""""

It was so sudden, so out of place, that all four of us simply froze.

Before us appeared a masked man. It was weird. He was dressed in such totally inappropriate clothing that you could only wonder what in the world he was thinking. The light of my lantern revealed a white button-down shirt (open), beach shorts, and sandals. He was dressed like a middle-aged guy stepping out to do some shopping...

"Surely it must be fate that has brought us together! Behold, our panoply of very useful and highly dungeon-friendly— Hmm?" The masked man had been about to spread out the cloth bundle he was carrying when he looked behind us and stopped. That reminded me that we were being chased.

"You have to run!" I shouted. "That thing—that *thing's* right behind us!"

"A Neroid! If it isn't a Hell Neroid! Why, what's something like that doing in a place like this?! Ahhh, there, there. Best you come here."

Hell Neroid...?

Ignoring our warning, the masked man went up to the..."Hell Neroid"...behind us, apparently not afraid of it at all. And the Hell Neroid, the impossible-to-describe life-form that had been chasing us, almost seemed to nuzzle up to his outstretched hand...

Chomp.

"Ahhhh! Your hand! Y-y-your hand, it—!"

"H-hey, bad Neroid, don't gnaw on my hand! That is *not* edible! Spit it out and return it to me this instant! Come on, spit! *Ptooie!* Right now! Right... Bah! *Vanir Death Ray!*"

As he shouted, a bright ray of light came from his right arm. It pierced the Hell Neroid, blowing it into a million pieces. The monster with whom we had fought and struggled so bitterly, he disposed of in the blink of an eye. Then he put the stump of his arm near the Neroid's remains and regenerated his hand, as if time were running in reverse.

I couldn't believe what I was seeing. I couldn't believe what I had just witnessed. He was clearly not human. But...

"What a poorly trained Neroid. Must have been wild. I can't imagine what a pet from Hell was doing here, though... Perhaps the sheer power of the mana in this dungeon accidentally opened a portal to Hell, and it wandered over?" The masked man *hmm*ed and muttered.

If nothing else, it was clear we owed our lives to this man who was not human. I felt obliged to say a word of thanks on behalf of my party, the rest of whom still hadn't figured out what was going on.

Before I could speak, though, the masked man dropped the bundle from his back and said, "Mm! Well, who cares about a wild Neroid anyway? Valued customers, we have a whole pile of items that should come in more than handy in a dungeon! And at special dungeon prices! Come, have a look!" He threw open the bundle, revealing the contents.

"A barrier stone! Look, he has a disposable barrier stone! Please, please let me have that! How much is the special dungeon price?!"

"Medicines and potions, too...! W-we're saved! The stairway to the twelfth floor is right here! If we take this stuff with us, we'll actually make it home!"

"Damn, he's even got food in there! That thing earlier ate our pack of food...! Thank the gods, we're saved...!"

My party members were rejoicing over the bounty in the masked man's bundle, buying one item after another. Who exactly was this guy?

"Thank you, thank you very much! Bwa-ha-ha-ha! This is my most profitable moment since I started this job! I should peddle my wares in this dungeon more often!" He was laughing uproariously as he sold off all his stock.

Seriously…who was this guy? He'd appeared as suddenly as a fresh breeze to bring us salvation in our moment of need. It was almost like he was…

"…A god…," I mumbled.

"Valued you may be, O customer, but even so, it's terribly rude to call me a god."

"Oh! I… I'm sorry…!" Apparently, I'd upset him with that word. Fair enough—a truly devout believer would be scandalized by being compared to a deity.

"Fantastic! I've sold every single thing I brought! Thank you, valued customers!"

"No, thank *you*, sir! If you hadn't shown up, we'd have been wiped out. These items really saved our skin! We owe you a lot!" Gil said. He was as thankful for the items as the masked man was satisfied to have sold them.

The masked man then stood up. "Think nothing of it. The health and safety of my customers is my foremost concern. Well then, I'll be off! Thank you for your patronage!"

And then, without so much as a light to see by, he walked off into the dungeon, until the only sign of him was the sound of his sandals slapping against the ground. We were left standing silently, until finally someone said:

"So what was that all about anyway?"

He'd left without even telling us his name… Was he some sort of dungeon fairy or something? No. I knew who he was, at least for me. "I give heartfelt thanks to the nameless god from who knows where…!"

3

"What's that rare monster want, wandering around in this dungeon? I'm done eating, and I want to get going."

"With that unusual outfit, Vanir certainly does look like some rare monster, doesn't he? I wonder why he likes that outfit so much...? I hope he doesn't meet any adventurers who accidentally attack him."

While I was having my snack break, Vanir had gone off somewhere. Wiz and I were hunkered down within a simple but effective barrier, which supposedly meant you could rest at ease, but even so, it was hard to relax in a dungeon. I actually wanted that weirdo "rare monster" to stay close.

Wiz patted her zombie dragon under the chin and said, "I do wonder where he's gone. Should we maybe shout for him? Of course, it could attract other monsters..." She trailed off. She was looking hard at the hallway in front of us.

Surprised, I looked, too. "Speaking of monsters...*that's* a monster...isn't it...?"

"I think so. Because no ordinary little girl could be down here in this dungeon."

A golden-haired girl had peeked around the corner ahead and was watching us.

Yeah, definitely not the sort of thing you normally saw in a dungeon. And yet...

"That's strange. My Sense Foe skill isn't reacting. Maybe she doesn't mean us any harm? But she could hardly be an adventurer at that age..."

"Doesn't mean us any harm? I wonder what kind of monster she would even be. She's not a ghost, and if she was a doppelgänger, she wouldn't spend her time watching us like that..."

So we had a little girl who didn't set off my Sense Foe ability. Wiz and I whispered to each other, never letting our guard down.

Then the little girl cocked her head. "Big Bro, Big Sis. Are you two bad adventurers? Or good adventurers?"

Wiz and I looked at each other.

"I guess if I had to, I'd say I'm a good adventurer," I said.

"I'm not an adventurer, but I'm not a bad Big Sis, I think," said Wiz, both of us still keeping a close eye on the girl, who was herself observing us from a distance.

This time, she smiled. "That's great. My name is Amaryllis! Say, won't you talk with me? It's lonely wandering around this dungeon all by myself for so long." She looked almost shy as she spoke.

"Sure, we can talk, but, Amaryllis, what are you doing down here alone? Are you, um…" I hesitated for a second. "Are you even human?"

A look of sadness passed over her face. "No, not anymore. The man who raised me was a wizard. He did magical research that turned me into a chimera. And now…I can't exactly live out in the open in town, so he told me to hide myself down in this dungeon. He said when he'd figured out how to fix me, he'd come get me. So I'm staying down here until he comes."

Geez, that was heavy. Wiz and I went silent.

After a moment, I said, "So, um… This man, what is he to you? Where are your mommy and daddy?"

"Mom and Dad died. The other man, he said he bought me. He made sure I had plenty to eat. He was so nice!"

…So she was supposed to hide down here while she waited? Didn't sound to me like that wizard had any intention of coming to get her. This girl Amaryllis had lost her parents, then been purchased for use in magical experiments, and finally abandoned in a dungeon. Talk about a buzzkill.

Suddenly, Wiz said, "In that case, let me make you better! I might not look like much, but I'm an amazing wizard myself—did you know that? I even knew a chimera once. I'm sure I can help you!" She smiled reassuringly.

…Damn. I was really starting to feel bad for underestimating this Lich for so long.

"R-really? You can actually turn me back to normal?"

"Yes, I mean it. So come over here; don't be afraid. This zombie dragon is my friend."

Wiz was trying to sound gentle, but Amaryllis still looked hesitant… "But, Sis, are you sure you won't be afraid when you see my body? You won't think it's…gross?" She was obviously feeling pretty uncomfortable.

"Don't worry—I'm even friends with ghosts and monsters. Don't be afraid, just come h—"

The words died in Wiz's throat as Amaryllis emerged into the hallway.

As for me, standing beside Wiz, I swallowed hard and felt like I might wet myself.

Amaryllis's head was attached to the body of a spider.

She scuttled closer on her spider legs with startling speed. "Big Siiiis!"

"Eeeyargh!" I howled and hid behind Wiz, who was just about weeping.

"H-h-h-hold on! A-A-Amaryllis, sweetie, just wait a second! Big Sis needs a minute to collect herself, okay?!"

"What's wrong, Sis? Sis, what's wrong? You said! You said you wouldn't be afraid! You said you'd fix me! You promised!" she cried, shaking her hair and nodding at us as she came closer.

I'm scared! What is this, a horror movie?!

"Just take it easy, little lady! Here, Big Bro's got some candy for you!"

"It's okay I swear your Big Sis isn't really scared and I will fix you I will help you so just please let's all calm down and wait wait wait please oh! Vanir! Vaniiiiiiir!"

"Ahhhh! I like kids, but young lady, you've got to slow doooooown!"

Wiz and I threw ourselves into each other's arms, shaking and crying.

"My word, it's gotten loud in here. Hmm? Is that you, Lady Amaryllis?"

It was Vanir, coming up behind us. At the sound of his voice, Amaryllis stopped where she was. "Oh? That beautiful mask... Is that you, Vanir? Fancy meeting you here so far down in this dungeon."

"".............................?"" Wiz and I, still hugging each other, turned slowly toward Vanir.

"Another excellent choice of appearance, my lady," he said. "I'm so sorry to interrupt you when you're feasting on such delectable fright, but these two are with me."

"Oh! Well, do pardon me. Wouldn't you know it—Stesky, my pet Hell Neroid, ran off. When I went after him, I discovered that the rich mana in this dungeon had connected a part of it to Hell... I came over here to look for him and bumped into these two, so I thought I'd just help myself to some bad vibes..."

Hey, hang on a second. "What? Amaryllis, alleged chimera child... You're actually a demon? So what was with that story about being turned into a chimera by a magical experiment?"

"Oh, that? I made that all up. I just *love* feelings of terror, and I chose this form out of personal preference. Ooh, well, anger and frustration are more Vanir's thing. You're very sweet, but I'll pass."

...I really, really hate demons.

4

"I'll be on my way, then. I have to go find Stesky... Oh yes, Vanir! Perhaps with your all-seeing powers, you could tell me where my pet is."

"Oh, um, we also must be going. Fare thee well, Lady Amaryllis! May we meet again in Hell!"

"Er... Oh..." Amaryllis looked a little taken aback by Vanir's evasive response, but nonetheless, she bowed to us, then scurried off down the hallway.

"Snf... Snrrrf," Wiz sniffled. "I'm glad... I'm glad she wasn't actually a forcibly augmented chimera... But still...I can't quite cope with this..."

Boy, did I know how she felt.

For that matter, I think I *did* wet myself a little.

"How long do you plan to continue sniffling and weeping? Listen, you two, we'll be going soon. Bwa-ha-ha-ha-ha! And anyway, you should rejoice, Wiz! For I have liquidated everything the young lad didn't buy from us! I think I may start coming to this dungeon from time to time to do some business!"

"…I think I'm starting to hate demons just a little bit…"

"…?! I object to your allowing the actions of that one demon to impact your opinion of the rest of us!"

—Floor 15—

"Please, Vanir, just a little! I don't need much, just a little bit!"

"Don't do it! MP is the source of all a demon's power and indeed of their very existence! H-hey, I said *don't* try to drain me! If you need to recover your MP, just suck some out of the next monster we meet!"

"But MP from dungeon monsters always makes my stomach feel bloated. Maybe it's all the mana they absorb! Surely just a little bit wouldn't hurt anything! Demons are supposed to have the highest-quality MP of all, right? Just a little! Just a fingertip's worth!"

"S-stop that—hands off my mask! Anyway, what's going on here? I've been wondering about the sheer quantity of monsters we've encountered. It's enough to run even a Lich like you out of MP in short order. Convenient as it is for the boy's leveling, I don't know why we should be encountering so many…"

Wiz and Vanir were arguing as I kept a lookout for monsters. "Y'know, you're right, we have been running into a lot of enemies. Way more than you ever would on the surface. I never dreamed my level would go up so much in one day."

I'd already reset my level twice and was on my third journey up the numbers. On the surface, it might have taken me half a day to hunt down five frogs. The encounter rate in this dungeon was definitely weird.

Then I noticed the rosary hanging from Wiz's neck (it was hard to miss it as she struggled with Vanir to Drain Touch some MP from him).

"It's got to be because of my rosary!" Wiz said. "They told me it would lead to a wonderful encounter, but they never mentioned it would even attract monsters in a dungeon… Ahhhhh! Vanir, stop! Give it back—don't throw it away!"

Geez, every single item she had in stock…

"Gah, I knew something was wrong…! I'll pin down the next monster we meet; then you absorb MP from it! Anyway, are you that desperate for an 'encounter'? I'm friends with a demon whose head isn't quite all there, but he's handsome enough. And quite loving. His name is Maxwell. He is from another world. Perhaps you'd like me to introduce you."

Wiz, still trying to grab the rosary back, started to fidget as if the idea wasn't entirely unappealing to her. "Loving and handsome, you say? …Er, well, if he's kind and devoted, I don't mind so much how he looks… When you say his head isn't quite all there, um, what do you mean exactly? He wouldn't happen to be any good with numbers, would he?"

"He's missing the entire back of his head."

"You mean his head *physically* isn't all there? No! I don't want someone like that! Wait, demons don't even have genders, do they?!"

Watching the two of them jabber, I had almost forgotten I was deep down in a deadly dungeon…

—Floor 17—

Seriously, how long had we been down here?

I was taking my second rest, but the constant state of heightened anxiety in a dungeon made it hard to know how much time had passed.

I'd drunk the fatigue-relief potion I'd bought from Vanir, so I wasn't actually feeling all that tired, but I was still a little out of it.

"Hmm? Getting tired, are you? I don't blame you; nearly an entire day has passed on the surface. Here, you had best drink this potion. It will dispel the sleepiness. It's a bam!-insta-wake potion."

"Vanir, you brought that?! But the side effects— Hrrrmf!" The way Vanir clapped his hand over Wiz's mouth before she could get out whatever she had been about to say made me hesitant to drink the potion he'd given me.

"So it's supposed to wake you up. What's it made of? It's not poisonous or anything, is it?"

"Oh, hardly. For someone as lucky as you, I doubt there will even *be* any side effects… Mm, yes, I see it; I can see it now: your future, you running around all energetic after drinking that potion."

"No more pranks like earlier, where you pretend I'm going to die or something, all right?" Sitting on the cold dungeon floor and full of trepidation, I brought the potion to my lips. Then I said, "I've saved up a pretty decent number of skill points. Why don't we go home? I came here to raise my level, not clear the whole dungeon."

Just then, Wiz finally managed to peel Vanir's hand off her mouth. "We can't stop now! We've come so far! Let's push that last little bit to the very end! The final chamber of a dungeon like this, the room where the master of the dungeon resides, usually has amazing loot and powerful equipment waiting inside! If you're going to try to take on the Demon King, don't you think that loot would come in handy?"

Oh yeah…the Demon King…

"I'll be honest with you: I haven't really decided yet if I'm actually going to fight him. Hey, aren't you both, like, friends of his? Could you live with yourselves if my party and I took him out?"

Wiz and Vanir had both been the Demon King's generals; surely they saw him from time to time.

The two of them traded a look, though, and Wiz said, "But being defeated is part of the Demon King's job description, isn't it?"

"Indeed. He crushes humanity under his heel, until at last a bold adventurer arises, they have a battle for the ages, and finally the king goes out in dramatic fashion. That's what it means to be the Demon King. Besides, he's getting on in years. He's probably thinking of having a proper send-off and passing the throne to his daughter."

I guess I didn't understand how demons thought.

That reminded me, though, of how Vanir wanted to build a dungeon. It wasn't his end goal, though. That was to be defeated by some adventurers, and in his last moments to savor their despair after they beat him... Kind of a pathetic dream, if you ask me. But maybe demons had their own way of living—their own aesthetics, if you will. I mean, after all, there was a whole village of Arch-wizards who had enough power among them that they seemed like they could take over the world if they really wanted to, but instead of even becoming adventurers, they were content to be cobblers or clothing-store proprietors or NEETs.

I'd known there were plenty of weirdos in this world, but this was ridiculous...

"So the Demon King is getting on in years, huh? But I mean, he's the king. He must still be the most powerful person in his own army, right? But...like, he's *just* strong enough that maybe even someone like me could take him on?"

"No, he's certainly not the strongest. I suspect his daughter is already more powerful than he is. I have no idea whether 'someone like you' could handle him, but he's still got enough spring in his step to crush an ogre's head with his bare hands."

Made sense, I guess. You wouldn't expect him to be a pushover.

"I sort of thought power was supposed to be everything in this world. Like it was just, *Yep! Strongest guy around is the Demon King! No question!*"

"Do you take us for meatheads? Or were the leaders of your world always the very strongest who could be found? I can't speak for the place you come from, but here, every Demon King in history has always possessed the following qualities if nothing else: first, charisma enough to attract distinctive generals to their army; second, power enough to keep their subordinates in line. They also need a fair degree of intelligence. But the charisma, the ability to attract generals with real talent, is probably the most important thing."

"I don't think this one managed it, judging by you and Wiz." Looking at these two, who were completely off doing their own thing, I even started to think that maybe it was harder than I'd realized to be the Demon King.

Vanir stood up, asking if I was done resting. "Whatever the case, even someone as puny as you could do with a little bit of equipment to give him a fighting chance in a battle. Although I personally hope for some very lucrative loot! Just you wait, Dungeon Master—we're coming to steal all your treasure! Bwa-ha-ha-ha-ha-ha!"

With this guy along, this felt less like an adventure and more like a burglary.

"Say, Kazuma, have you been thinking about what kinds of skills you want to acquire? I can teach you Teleport when we leave this dungeon."

Teleport! Man, I really wanted that ability. It seemed like it would be useful in all sorts of scenarios.

"Crimes involving magic, including Teleport and light-bending spells, are punished far more severely than ordinary offenses," Vanir said.

"…?! I d-d-d-didn't say a word! I was just thinking about how useful Teleport might be, that's all! Like, say you get into a real tight spot at the Demon King's castle; you could just run away again, right?!"

"If you're hoping to use Teleport to escape from the castle, you'll somehow have to neutralize the barrier around it. That being the case, perhaps you'd like to learn one of my skills? I have death rays, eye beams…"

"I'm just a human. If I fired a *death* ray…"

"It would kill you, of course. But think about it: a last-ditch ace in the hole that also kills the user? Imagine how surprised your opponent would be! There are few performances that demonstrate such wholehearted devotion!"

"Unlike a certain goddess, I haven't sold my soul to party tricks!"

5

—Floor 18—

"*Vanir Death Ray*! *Vanir Death Ray*! Vanir... Arrrgh, there are so many of them! Wiz, can't you do something about this?! This is becoming tiresome—just blow them away with Explosion!"

"N-no, I shouldn't use Explosion in here! The entire dungeon would come down on our heads... Oh! Eek, those nasty minotaurs are ganging up on my sweet zombie dragon!"

"Whoa, hey?! Hey, one's coming this way! The monster's coming over to meeeee!"

We were suddenly in a very, very tight spot. When we'd come down the stairs, we'd found ourselves in a monster nest. Vanir and Wiz couldn't corral all of them alone, and one of the minotaurs started edging its way toward me...

"*Bumooooo!*"

"Eep!" I quickly ducked, and the monster's ax passed just a few inches over my head. If I'd been even a second slower, I wouldn't have a head anymore. And without Aqua here, if I died, that was it for me.

Dammit! Dungeons are scary! Monsters are scary! My heart is going a mile a minute!

I guess that's how it usually works in battle. If you die, you're dead. I found myself belatedly very, very thankful for Aqua. Back when she and I had first gotten here, I felt like a kid who'd gotten a robot tanuki from the future only to discover that the fourth-dimensional pocket was sold separately. But the next time I saw her, maybe I'd be a little nicer.

Vanir and Wiz had their hands full trying to keep the horde of monsters at bay. I would have to deal with the bullheaded giant myself. I looked up at it—it was several times my size—and drew my katana, all the while getting ready to run.

"Dammit, of all the times to realize how much I appreciate having Aqua around! I can't die here! I've got to get Aqua back, and then I'm going to live a pleasant, dissolute life for the rest of my days! Waking up at noon, drinking all day, lying around, going out at night—maybe we can even take a trip all together! I'm supposed to be an adventurer, and I've hardly been anywhere in this world!"

"He admitted it!" Wiz shouted. "Vanir, did you hear that? Kazuma is never able to admit how he truly feels, but he just did! Unbelievable! To realize your true feelings in the direst of straits, how romanti— Agh?!"

I didn't know what she was going on about, but one of the minotaurs smashed its ax into her head, sending her flying.

"Geez! Wiz?!" I glanced away from my own opponent for a second, but Wiz got up as if nothing had happened.

"Now I *have* to make sure that you and Lady Aqua are reunited, so you can acknowledge your love for each other! Vanir, I'm about to use a whole lot of magic, so promise me you'll give me plenty of MP after this battle!"

Wiz, clearly laboring under some sort of misunderstanding, was being beaten up by minotaurs and attacked from every direction, but it didn't even seem to bother her as she intoned some sort of spell. I'd always known Liches weren't affected by non-magical attacks, but watching her shrug off blow after blow was incredible, nonetheless.

Beside me, three zombie dragons squared off with more minotaurs. As for Vanir, he was drawing something on the ground using the blood of the minotaur he'd just slain…

"*Bumoooo!*" the monster across from me bellowed and raised its ax.

"F-fine, just try me, you—!"

Not missing a beat, I jumped in with Chunchunmaru and slashed at the minotaur's legs. But I was and had always been very weak, and my attack just sort of scratched it. My level was over 30 already. It kind of ticked me off that I couldn't do anything to it!

The minotaur looked like it was going to bring its weapon down on my head, but…it never happened.

"*Petrification*!"

The minotaur across from me turned to stone, presumably thanks to Wiz's spell. And not just the one in front of me—most of the monsters around us were immediately petrified.

"Bwa-ha-ha-ha-ha-ha-ha! You do know how to handle yourself, Wiz! Well, I won't let you have all the fun! I, Vanir, Duke of Hell, command: Come forth from Hell, my servants!" Still cackling, Vanir placed his hand on the magic circle drawn in minotaur blood at his feet. The gory diagram began to glow with an eerie light…

When it faded, there was a group of creatures with devils' bodies and bat-like wings. If you looked in the dictionary under the word *demon*, this was what you would expect to find.

Suddenly confronted by a small army of demons, the minotaurs and then every other monster nearby started fleeing in panic. I felt a touch of terror myself, to see what this normally laid-back demon could do when he really wanted to…

"Gosh, Lord Vanir. You can't go summoning us out of the blue like that. We're busy as hell down there!"

"Yeah, you're the one who abandoned your territory to go play around on the surface and left us to pick up the slack!"

"Uh…Lord Vanir? What's with the outfit? I don't think that's how a Duke of Hell normally…"

The demons didn't sound very happy. They all had horrific appearances, but I wasn't scared of any of them in the least.

We and our crew of demons and undead marched through the dungeon like a conquering army. The monsters we ran into were not creatures I could have made a dent in even if I'd tried. We're talking enemies so big and bad that if I hadn't been surrounded by this entire crew, I would have wet my pants at the mere sight of them.

One after another, Wiz simply transformed them into undead, further increasing our strength, until we finally arrived at…

—Floor 20—

This floor didn't look like the others. The walls glowed with a faint light. Maybe they were imbued with magic, or maybe there was luminescent moss growing on them or something.

Strangely, I hadn't sensed any monsters ever since we arrived on this floor. Maybe only the Dungeon Master was allowed down here.

Now we stood before the final room, the boss chamber. It had a thick door engraved with terrible decorations, like it belonged to the last boss in some video game. The Dungeon Master had to be on the other side.

I nodded to Vanir and Wiz, and we slowly pushed open the door. Inside we found...

"How very good of you to make it this far! I give you my grudging compliments for surviving my dungeon to reach me here. Now, show me your strength! For I am the King of the Undead, possessor of immortality! A thousand years I have waited, and now I will show you what I, the primogenitor of the vampires, can truly...truly...!"

The Dungeon Master was sitting, almost relaxed, on an ostentatious throne in the middle of the room, but as he saw us, he trailed off. As he saw the two people behind me, specifically.

"Gosh, I didn't know Liches had been demoted and *vampires* had become the Kings of the Undead. When did that happen? And you're right, it *was* a lot of trouble getting here. Hoo-hoo-hoo, ha-ha-ha-ha-ha!"

"Bwa-ha-ha-ha-ha-ha-ha! Bwa-ha-ha-ha-ha-ha-ha! Bwa-ha-ha-ha-ha-ha! My goodness, but this is a sprawling dungeon you've made! Quite a project for a fledgling chick a mere thousand years old! Bwa-ha-ha-ha-ha-ha-ha-ha-ha-ha-ha-ha!"

Vanir, who'd used no small amount of MP himself shooting death rays at everything on the way here, started cackling.

The Dungeon Master froze in front of me. "Ahem... I'll put tea on, my dear visitors, and then perhaps we can discuss the reason for your... visit...?" He was trying his damnedest to smile, but he looked like he might cry.

Gee, I...I felt kind of bad for him.

6

"Bwa-ha-ha-ha-ha-ha-ha! Bwa-ha-ha-ha-ha-ha-ha!"

"Oh! This is legendary magical power! This magical item has legendary-level power!"

Vanir and Wiz were deep in the Dungeon Master's room, crowing over the treasure. The vampire and I sipped our tea and watched.

"Uh… Sorry about my companions," I said.

"No, no, it is I who should apologize. A pathetic worm of a vampire should never have dared to make such a grand dungeon. After you've all finished here, I think I'll go back to the country and live a modest life growing tomatoes or something."

The *original* vampire was going to live out in the country and grow tomatoes? I couldn't imagine the vampires' hatred of sunlight was very conducive to farmwork, but…wow.

"Yeah. That might be a good idea. Then you wouldn't have to deal with this kind of stuff."

"Yes, if I'm going to have to endure terror like this, I'd rather live quietly and easily somewhere. I've been alive for a millennium now, but I never imagined I would find myself surrounded by such a panoply of demons and undead. Not to mention that great undead, a Lich, and a demon who's been around far longer than I have. I'm counting myself lucky that I wasn't destroyed outright."

And then the thousand-year-old bloodsucker sipped his tea again, observing Vanir and Wiz with detachment.

"Bwa-ha-ha-ha-ha-ha! What a great haul of silver and gold! Between this and what I'll make when the kid buys what he promised, I can start doing some *real* business! I've got it! How about a casino? Wiz, I'm taking this loot, and I'm going to build a casino! A magnificent gambling palace that will surpass even the great nation of Elroad!"

"Ohhhhh! Look, Vanir, just look at this! It's bursting with magic! I don't know what it does, but it feels powerful enough to turn the world inside out…!"

I couldn't help wondering why the vampire, who sat delicately drinking his tea, looked so much more like a proper big bad than the two rifling through his treasure with greed in their eyes.

Now that the vampire had surrendered, Wiz had released her zombie dragons to pass on to the next life, and Vanir had sent his lackeys home. As the vampire and I engaged in pleasant conversation, Wiz and Vanir were packing up the treasure he'd offered them to spare his life, stuffing it all into Vanir's carrying cloth.

"Ahhh! This will never do; there's too much treasure here! We will never be able to carry all this home!"

"That is a problem, Vanir. Whatever shall we do? Each item here possesses such powerful magic. I'd really like to take them all with me if I could…"

They stared right at the vampire as they spoke.

G-geez, you guys aren't satisfied just breaking in and stealing all his stuff? You have to make him help you carry it, too?

"I'll have Wiz teach me Teleport right now, and I'll register this dungeon's lowest floor as one of my destinations. That good enough for you?" I said.

Evidently it was, because Vanir and Wiz came over with something in their arms. A pitch-black sword and a set of full armor (also black), both obviously of extremely fine make.

"Take this, my boy. I believe it may be the strongest magical sword in this entire treasure hoard. You could sell it for a small fortune, but at the moment, I believe it would benefit you even more to use it yourself."

"And I think this armor is quite something," Wiz added. "I can feel powerful magic coming from it. If you were to wear it, I don't think you would have any problems on the way to the Demon King's castle."

They both gave me the items without batting an eyelash. Even though they were probably each worth a whole heap of money. Say what you would about them, maybe they really did have my best interests at heart. Feeling almost a little embarrassed, I put the armor on…

*   *   *

"...Um, it's too heavy for me to move."

...and found that as soon as I equipped a single gauntlet, I was rooted to the spot.

What was going on here? This was weird. I know I was a member of the weakest class, but after having my level reset several times and working myself hard down here in this dungeon, I was up above Level 30. And unlike the last time I'd tried to upgrade my equipment, I was confident that I had the muscles for it now...

"Oh, that armor is for Crusaders only. And incidentally, the sword there can only be used by Sword Masters," said the vampire (whose name we still didn't know).

What did he mean, "only"? Were members of the weakest class not allowed to use legendary equipment, either?

"You wouldn't, er, happen to have any powerful equipment that's meant for Adventurers, would you?"

"I-I'm sorry—nobody wants to be an Adventurer, so no one makes powerful weapons or armor for them... At least, I certainly don't have any...," the vampire said.

When Vanir heard our conversation, he burst out laughing. "Bwa-ha-ha-ha-ha-ha-ha, bwaaaaa-ha-ha-ha-ha-ha! O boy who cannot seem to become a hero for the life of him, is this not ideal? This is itself what makes you unique! Your weak equipment, your motley collection of skills! If you were to take them and face the Demon King, I'm sure you would be called one of the greatest heroes ever to live! I see it; I can see it! A future in which you are given a nickname such as Harem Guy or the Strongest of the Weakest! Waaaaa-ha-ha-ha-ha-ha!"

After we got back to town and I picked up some skills, one of the first things I wanted to do was beat this guy up.

"Dammit, what the hell? Hmm, but if it's for Crusaders... It's all black and kind of...scary, but maybe it would make a good souvenir for

Darkness. You don't happen to have any wizard staffs or anything in there, do you?"

"Ooooh, I'm afraid I don't really have much of anything for wizards. Ah, but this ring I'm wearing increases the wearer's magical power. Would you like it?"

The vampire went to take the ring off his finger, but I quickly stopped him. "N-no, no, it's all right. I don't like feeling like I've robbed you blind. I'm sorry, it must seem to you like we're just here to loot your place."

"Oh, not at all; dungeons exist to be plundered. All the treasure I have here once belonged to some adventurer who tried their hand at my labyrinth. Don't give it a second thought. This ring, though—it's something I've cherished since the days of my mortal life, so I must admit I'm relieved."

He smiled a little, looking really pleased, when…

"Did you say a ring that increases magical power?" Wiz greedily slipped it onto her finger and stared at it.

…*Please, please stop.*

7

By the time we Teleported back to town, it was pitch-dark outside. We'd spent more than an entire day in that dungeon, and my sense of time was all out of whack.

"It's unlikely there are any carriages running at this hour. The fatigue-recovery and stimulant potions may have kept you going, but all that abrupt leveling up combined with a sustained state of heightened anxiety and a full day of battling will have taken a significant toll on your body. For today, go and get some rest. Tomorrow, you can learn your skills, then head out on your journey. That would be best." Vanir's carrying cloth was stuffed with treasure, and he was still holding a full armload of loot, too.

I, carrying only the suit of armor for Darkness, said thanks to Vanir and Wiz. "You were both a huge help. I promise I'm gonna go get that idiot back."

"When it comes to that goddess, eh, I could take her or leave her."

"Well, I couldn't! Kazuma… If and when the time comes, we'll be giving the defense of this town a little help from the wings. You can go on your journey with peace of mind. We'll make sure Lady Aqua has a home to return to. When you get back, I'll be more than happy to help you raise your level again or do whatever you need."

I think I'd had enough of that. Frankly, that dungeon had been terrifying. Being surrounded by powerful monsters had activated a primal terror as a living being, and I still hadn't stopped shaking. I thought I might have a little trauma around dungeons after this.

"Yes, there's still loot left in that dungeon. I know you must go on your journey now; we can collect the rest after you get back. So make sure you *do* get back. I don't look forward to having to march all the way back down twenty tedious floors again otherwise."

What a very Vanir-esque way to send me off.

"When you get home, I'll teach you Advanced Magic for real. So please come back safely!" Wiz smiled kindly. Earlier, I'd tried to learn Advanced Magic along with Teleport, but I hadn't been able to do it. I'd had enough skill points, but it refused to show up in my Available Skills field. With Basic Magic, all you had to do was shout the name of the spell. For Intermediate Magic, there was a process, but not much of one. Even an amateur could manage those, but when it came to Advanced Magic…

"For Advanced Magic, you have to learn specific gestures and incantations for each spell and even the right flow of MP," Wiz explained. "I doubt you could pick it all up in a single day… Oh! But if you're interested in Explosion, I know you've seen Megumin using it every day for quite a long time, right? So you could—"

"Don't need it."

Anyway, even if I did learn Explosion, I would never have enough

MP to use it. Even Megumin, an Arch-wizard and a member of the Crimson Magic Clan, who were all bursting with MP, only had enough to use it once a day.

Still… Advanced Magic when I got home, huh? I wanted that spell that turned you invisible—*really* wanted it. Not that I'd given any thought yet to what I would use it for, of course…

"I see it. I can see the future! I see you learning Advanced Magic, turning yourself invisible, and going to the public b—"

"Welp, nice work today! I'll drop by the shop again before I leave tomorrow!"

It was almost dawn.

"I was sure the waiting area for the carriages was around here... Did they move it when I wasn't looking?"

I was trying to find where I could catch a carriage. I'd gotten so caught up in my trip down memory lane that I'd lost track of time and missed the midnight departure.

I had the best sense of direction of anyone in our party; it was unthinkable that I would get lost. Which meant they must have changed the place from which the carriages departed.

It was always the same story. We'd be on a quest, and the moment I took my eyes off those three kids, they would all disappear. I was sure that if they tried to come after me, they'd just get lost on the way; it would be a rough journey. I wondered what to do. Should I wait to leave on my trip until after I made sure the others had all grown up into fully matured human beings?

It happened just then, as I was wandering around looking for the carriages and mulling over my duties as the party's guardian.

"Lady Aqua? Where are you going dressed like that?"

The voice from behind me belonged to my adorable follower Cecily.

"What a coincidence meeting you here at this hour, Cecily," I said. "No… It can't be just chance."

It was true: Cecily was a distinguished Axis disciple. She must have sensed the holy war that was about to begin; that was what had drawn her here so early in the morning.

"No, no… I was arguing with a tavern keeper. It was closing time, but I didn't want to leave. And before I knew it, it was almost dawn. Incidentally, that's where I was drinking, over there." She pointed to a bar I'd been to several times myself. I thought I remembered it being in a livelier part of town than this, but maybe it wasn't just the carriage depot; maybe the tavern had moved without my realizing it, too.

"Drinking? Yes, I understand. When I hear the words *last call*, I just get so frantic. It's a battle to the death after that. But then usually Kazuma comes to get me after they complain to him."

"I know exactly what you mean, Lady Aqua. When I get drunk, I just want to get drunker and louder, and it drives me frantic when they want me to go home instead."

She truly was an Axis follower: This was someone who *got* me.

"By the way, the bar said I didn't have to pay; they just begged me not to come back…," Cecily added.

"I see, so the barkeep is a *tsundere*. They would never *actually* want to ban pure, righteous Axis followers from their establishment. Her actions just *scream tsundere*. You should make sure to drop in more often."

"I'll do just that, Lady Aqua! Ahem, to go back to my question, why do you look like that?" Cecily asked, smiling brightly.

"Hear me, O Axis believer Cecily. I mourn for this world. People living good, upright lives are oppressed by the awful Demon King. And I intend to pull that source of evil up by the roots!"

"Y-you do?! You mean, Lady Aqua, you yourself are going to defeat him? What about Megu-tan?! I don't see her anywhere! Ahem, I mean, where are Megumin and Kazuma and even that…grrr…that one other girl, the Eris-loving Crusader?!"

I wasn't sure when Megumin had evolved into Megu-tan, and it sort of bugged me, but nonetheless I said, "This journey is going to be a cruel one. I decided those three fledglings simply don't have the strength. Therefore…I shall go alone to defeat the Demon King!"

"No, you can't…! Lady Aqua, forgive poor, lowly Cecily for offering her opinion, but I think it might be best for you to bring those three along. Otherwise, they'll only lecture you whether you win or lose, won't they?"

Lecture me whether I win or lose?

"Ooh, I wonder what I should do… Maybe a good souvenir would help…"

"I'm afraid I doubt it, milady."

I very nearly said that I would just put off hunting down the Demon King, but I didn't let the words out. Bah, she might not know who I truly was, but I wasn't about to let myself look pathetic in front of one of my followers.

"Say, Lady Aqua, what do you intend to do next?"

"Good question. First, I'm going to catch a carriage to somewhere cold. The Demon King's castle seems like the sort of thing that would be built in a cold place, doesn't it? You know, the north or somewhere like that."

"Very well, Lady Aqua. Poor lowly Cecily will accompany you as far as she can."

Ahhh, my devoted Axis follower. She really must have sensed the imminent holy war, and it had inspired her.

"If you insist, then I suppose I have to let you tag along. Come on, Cecily—we're going somewhere cold!"

"Roger that, Lady Aqua. But first, maybe we could ask the carriage people to take us in the direction of the Demon King's castle. They're professional drivers, after all. I'm sure they have a sense of the right way to go."

Ah, Cecily. So intelligent. I'd known her for a long time now. Maybe it would be safe to tell her the truth. "I always knew you were capable, Cecily. As a reward, I may eventually reveal my true self to you…"

"No, you can't!" she cried, sounding oddly nervous.

Ah, my humble follower, so free of any desire!

1

"I'm home!"

""Welcome back!""

When I opened the front door, Megumin and Darkness were there, sitting on the carpet looking like they'd been waiting for me for quite a while.

"So you've made it safely home. I thought you would simply duck into the dungeon and grind a few levels, so when you didn't come home for an entire day, I started to worry," Megumin said warmly.

"No kidding! I *told* you you should let me come along to play defense for you. And here you've got… What *is* that?" Before Darkness could really get into it, I'd held out the suit of armor, bringing her up short.

"A souvenir. Powerful armor. They said only Crusaders could use it, so I brought it back for you."

"Wow, class-restricted equipment. Items that can only be worn by a specific class are often very famous or important objects. Did you not find anything for yourself, Kazuma?" Megumin asked.

"Nah, they said Adventurer-only items don't really exist, since there's never any demand for 'em."

Hands trembling, Darkness took the armor and hugged it close. Her face was red, and her eyes were moist. "Thank you… I'll treasure

it." The words were so simple but so full of gratitude. Now I couldn't exactly tell her that I'd just gone ahead and brought it back because *I* couldn't use it.

"Pitch-black armor? Most appropriate for someone named Darkness, I should say."

"Totally. Especially with that color and the whole, y'know, style, though, I think she'll sort of look like she belongs with the Demon King."

"Eek… I'm not sure a paladin should be wearing black armor, but, well, it is what it is… Besides, this armor is really pretty. Powerful enchanted armor usually adjusts itself to fit the wearer. Maybe it'll change to look a little more knightly when I put it on." She carried the armor into the living room and gave it a quick polish with a dry cloth. She looked like she was genuinely enjoying herself as the rag squeaked along the armor.

Then Megumin tugged on my sleeve. "And where is my souvenir?"

"I, uh…don't have one for you."

I had a light meal and a bath, but when I got out of the tub, I didn't see Darkness anywhere. She'd really seemed taken with that armor; maybe she was in her room trying it on. Megumin was relaxing on the sofa, almost as if she'd been waiting for me to finish my bath. Even though it was late, she wasn't wearing her pajamas; instead, she had on her black one-piece.

"I'm gonna hit the sack. Busy day tomorrow," I said. "I don't know where you plan to go dressed like that, but don't stay up too late, huh?"

Tomorrow, I would go around to the adventurers Megumin and Darkness had rounded up while I was in the dungeon and learn some useful skills. As soon as I'd learned everything I needed, I would set out after Aqua. My travel bag was packed and ready to go, sitting in a corner of the living room. I guess Darkness and Megumin had gotten it together while I was out raising my level.

"That is a good point," Megumin said. "I suppose I shall go to bed, too, then." She stood up. And then, for some reason, she followed me right to my room.

I opened the door, and Megumin came in after me as if it was the most natural thing in the world.

. . . .

"Uh, what are you doing? I thought you were going to bed."

"Oh, I am. With you, Kazuma."

...*Huh?*

While I stood there frozen, Megumin walked over to the bed and patted the sheets. "This trip will be more dangerous than any other we've yet undertaken. So...I just want to make sure neither of us has any regrets before we leave."

She smiled just a little.

. . . . *Huh?!*

2

"U-uh, well, now that we're here, I d-do suppose I am a little nervous. Are you all right? You're not uncomfortable or anything?"

"Y-yeah, I'm fine, no problem. Same goes for you, Megumin. Don't overdo it, okay?"

There was no moon out tonight. The only light that leaked in through the window was the faint illumination of streetlamps lit by Axel's wizards. There wasn't enough light for me even to see Megumin's pale skin very clearly. And my Second Sight skill allowed me to make out only the outlines of things, like thermography. Even in the darkness, though, I could see those crimson eyes glowing clearly.

Megumin was lying on the bed, smiling gently up at me. So this was why she'd changed into her fancy dress.

The truth was, I was trying to distract myself, but the lower half of my body was hard to ignore. It was hard, all right...really hard. I wanted to hurry up and do something. Megumin must have noticed me looking at her dress, because she said, "This is the one outfit I own that is remotely sexy... What do you think? Is it all right? I mean, is it...?"

"Y-yeah, it's okay—I mean, it's pretty and, uh, turns me on and stuff."

"T-turns you on...? You couldn't come up with another— No, that's very Kazuma-ish." She chuckled softly. Then, still smiling, she opened her arms as if to welcome me into them. "It can't be easy for you. And that's okay. I'll accept all of you. I want us to have no regrets, to leave nothing undone. Do *whatever* you like, okay?"

Talk like that pushed me right up to the limit. If I backed down after an invitation like that, it would make me look almost as crazy as Megumin acted sometimes.

I worked my way on top of her, being careful not to lean too much of my weight on her, and Megumin wrapped her arms around me. One of the shoulder straps of her dress had slipped off, and maybe my eyes were adjusting to the darkness, because I felt like I could see her pale, exposed shoulder with impossible clarity.

You know, Darkness and I had only ever kissed. Maybe that was where I should start.

I brushed Megumin's cheek with my hand, and she placed her hand on top of mine, her eyes crinkling into a comfortable smile. That simple gesture was enough to set my nerves and excitement to MAX. Girls were such cheaters! This was already practically enough to push me over the edge.

As Megumin continued to stroke my hand placidly, I leaned my face closer to hers. She saw what I was trying to do, swallowed gently, and closed her eyes. Unlike the time Darkness kissed me, when she'd ambushed me, we both knew what was going to happen here. Sure, I was nervous, but I also sort of felt like I had to hurry up. Otherwise, we'd be interrupted, just like we always were at moments like this.

Yeah...right at the best part, that idiot would...!

That idiot...

*   *   *

"...? What's the matter?" Megumin opened one eye and stole an uneasy glance at me when she realized I wasn't kissing her.

That idiot wasn't going to come interrupt us. She couldn't. She wasn't even here right now.

In other words, this was my chance. Our chance. Finally, at long last, we had our chance... That was the normal way to think about this, right?

"I'm sorry," I said after a moment.

"Am I...not good enough? I know I'm not as well-endowed as Darkness or Aqua, but I do think I have a decent figure. Would you like to see it?"

"Believe me, I would *love* to— Wait, that's not the point. I want to do it. I *really* do. The lower half of me is about to go berserk. So I promise, it's not about whether you're attractive or not, Megumin. But..."

I couldn't believe what I was doing. I was throwing it all away. It was ridiculous, stupid. But...

"I want Aqua and Darkness to be around. I'd rather have everyone under one roof and constantly be wondering when they're going to burst in on us. I'd rather sneak into your room wondering when that idiot is going to find us. I know we always end up with someone barging in on us just at the best moment, but even then—"

I couldn't finish, because Megumin wrapped her arms around my neck and pressed her mouth against mine, kissing me passionately. I felt her tongue work its way into my mouth, and then I couldn't think of anything else at all. I began to draw her closer to me.

Just as I was about to go further, Megumin pulled her mouth away, rested her head on my chest, and: "That's what I love about you," she said. "How considerate you are... I love it so much, I can't stand it."

I could feel the warmth of her breath, her hand stroking the back of my head affectionately. Feeling her softness against my cheeks, I couldn't stand it anymore...!

*   *   *

"When we finally get Aqua back—that night, you and I are going to do something unbelievable. I promise, all right?"

She whispered the words into my ear, then gently pushed me back and slid out of the bed.

...*Huh?*

Um, maybe I wasn't one to talk, but Megumin's kiss had really gotten me going. Like, forget about Aqua—the desire to continue was winning out.

As I lay there feeling like I might burst into tears, Megumin stood with her hands clasped behind her back and gave me a teasing smile. "That moment when you said you were sorry, Kazuma, I felt so anxious until you told me why. So I thought I would tease you back just a little."

Tease me back? You mean get me in the mood? This was beyond teasing, or at least, I thought so. Hell, even if I went out for some succubus service now, they'd probably all be away on jobs at this hour.

Dammit, Massive Disappointment Megumin just got meaner and meaner.

"Uh, I...I apologize for that, so maybe we could keep going just a little bit..."

"Wh-why, you...! I wish you could just continue to act cool all the way through... Ahem, on that note." Megumin didn't leave my room but, for some reason, went and stood in front of the closet. "On that note, Darkness, you can stop hiding in there, all twitchy and fidgety, and go back to your own room!"

"Ahhh!" someone cried as Megumin opened the closet door with a slam. It was Darkness, sitting there blushing furiously. Who knows how long she had been there or why? "H-h-h-how did you know?"

"How did I know you were there, you mean? Because last night you were beside yourself with worry when Kazuma didn't come home, but tonight you darted upstairs before he even got out of the bath! Need I remind you that Crimson Magic Clan members have extremely high Intelligence? More than enough to see through the lustful, oversexed mind of someone like you, Darkness!"

"O-oversexed…! W-w-well, look who's talking, Megumin…!" Darkness was still seated inside the closet, and still blushing, and was now also shaking in fear.

Megumin dragged her out into the room. "I did not get a souvenir, so I came to take one for myself. As for you, I presume you were so excited by your present of a suit of armor, and so inflamed by last night's feelings of loneliness, that you came in here to set an ambush! Then, when you heard my voice, you panicked and hid in the closet!"

"H-how did you guess? That's exactly what happened. I was going to thank him for the armor…" Darkness was still blushing, and now she looked like she might cry, too.

"To repay a gift with your body…you depraved woman! I am happy with the simple act of embracing Kazuma, but what about you? You intended to give him your body, then say condescendingly, *Here, this is your reward!* Is that it? Have you that much confidence in yourself?!"

"I w-w-w-wasn't— I don't—! N-no, that wasn't what I was g-going to do!"

Megumin began to drag Darkness, looking close to tears, out of the room. "Then, as you peeped at Kazuma and me, you began to get excited yourself, and look at you now! How perverted this girl is! Come on—don't just sit there all night, panting like a beast in heat—we're going back to our rooms!"

"Hold on! You're way more pervy than I am, Megumin! You did all that stuff even though you *knew* I was there! Ahhh! Hey, I'm not done…!"

Megumin pulled Darkness all the way out of the room, and then they were gone.

Um… What about my *excitement?*

3

The next morning. We got to the carriage depot to find a long line of adventurers. Vanir and Penguin Suit were standing at the head of the queue.

"What is the matter, Kazuma? You're zoning out. You'll hurt yourself, trying to learn skills in that state."

"Er, right. Sorry."

We were about to set off after Aqua and pick a fight with the Demon King. When we'd left the house, I'd glanced back, thinking it might be the last time I ever saw the place, and I noticed something strange. A little girl waving good-bye to us from the second-floor balcony. It must have been the ghost of the noblewoman Aqua had mentioned, the one who lived in our mansion.

By the time I rubbed my eyes and looked again, she was gone, but maybe I really had seen her: I saw strange things sometimes. It seemed to be an aftereffect of having briefly been a follower of Regina. It was weird, though. The ghost girl didn't inspire terror or even unease in me. She was who I'd been thinking about just now.

"Boy," Vanir interrupted me. "Or should I say, valued customer. I sure made a killing this morning. It's the biggest deal I've done since I started Vanir's Magical Item Shoppe. I haven't been able to stop laughing since. You can leave looking after the house to me—I will take good care of your Dark God and your chicken nugget. You may depart this world with a calm heart."

"Uh, you mean depart on my *trip*, right? You know what? Never mind. What did you say you would take good care of? The chicken nugget thing I get, but what was the other one?"

Vanir had Chomusuke in one hand and Emperor Zel in the other. Penguin Suit—that is to say, Zeeleschilt—turned to me, ignoring my question as he gave me a quick pat on the back. "Boy, I owe you for protecting me from various villainous goddesses on many an occasion. If, perchance, you should find yourself bereft of life on your journey, come to my fief in Hell. I shall receive you lavishly."

"Please, you're gonna give me bad luck…"

Zeeleschilt was pretty much the mascot of Wiz's store these days, but this was a reminder that he was still a demon—and I guess he was trying to encourage me, in his demonic way.

"All right. You ready to learn some skills, Kazuma?" Dust stepped forward from among the adventurers and pointed his sword at me.

He wasn't trying to make fun of me. I really was going to learn skills from all these people. And Dust wasn't the only person I knew here. The line was full of people I'd met and gotten close to over the last year or so.

"You're about to go toe to toe with the Demon King, so we're gonna beat the crap out of y— Er, I mean, we're gonna give you the training of a lifetime. Consider it our parting gift."

"Did you almost say *beat the crap out of you*? And anyway, no way I'm going toe to toe with the Demon King, or storming the castle, or anything! Goal number one is to bring Aqua back!"

As I railed at Dust, Megumin and Darkness stood to either side of me, smiling and nodding as if I were nothing more than a temperamental child. The two of them had their hearts set on a frontal assault on the Demon King. Me, I felt priority one was to link up with Aqua. If we could do that, I didn't really care what else happened.

At this point, though, even a coward like me was bracing himself. I'd acquired lots of skill points. I was like the main character experiencing his awakening in the climactic part of a story. To gain the peaceful future I'd always wanted, I would destroy the Demon King's army with all my strength.

The gathered adventurers took an uneasy step back when they saw me grin.

"Say, Kazuma, you sure you don't want to nix that trip?"

"Yeah, you've always been a little strange, but it's worse than usual today."

The other adventurers sounded worried, but I didn't blame them: They didn't know that I'd awakened to my true power.

"I appreciate your concern, but I'm now one of the most capable people in Axel. Leave Aqua and the Demon King to me. You just make sure this town's still standing when we get back. My mansion's here, after all." Then I gave a pointed snort—and for some reason, everybody grimaced.

"'One of the most capable people in Axel,' my foot! This from the guy who supposedly did all his power-leveling in a dungeon with Wiz and Vanir babysitting him!"

"Yeah, he's just cobbled those levels together by paying for them! And you have the nerve to act all high-and-mighty?!"

"Nice attitude when we're all about to teach you our skills, Mr. Weakest Class!"

It wasn't just their voices the adventurers raised; they all held up their weapons menacingly. Oops, just when it had seemed like they were worried about me, now they were enraged by me.

"I'm swimming in skill points and past Level 30! They say when you get to 30, you're a veteran. I'm not like you shrimps cooling your heels in Axel! Now, step up and teach me those skills!"

"You think you're hot stuff just 'cause you got a few levels! You wanna learn some skills so badly? Let me show you how they work…by testing them out on you!"

"*You're* the shrimp! We know all about how you got chased around by that frog just the other day! If you want to learn so badly, let me drop some intermediate magic on you!"

"Do it! If he can't handle us, he'll never be able to beat the Demon King anyway! C'mon, everybody—I've found our new punching bag!"

The adventurers were razzing me and flipping me off with every middle finger available. What a bunch of short tempers. Bastards!

"Fine, before I get to the Demon King, I'll warm up on you!

So bring on every skill I don't already know! The name's Kazuma Satou! Bring it oooooonnnnnn!"

Everyone else leered at me...then they took me at my word and all attacked at once!

4

"I'm sorry, Kazuma, but there's so much of it, it's going to take a while to— What happened here?!" Wiz, clutching a huge bag, cried out when she saw the crowd of adventurers laid out on the ground left, right, and center around the carriage depot.

"Oh, sorry, Wiz. I didn't know you were going to bring that for me."

"It's fine, but...what in the world is going on?! I thought you were going to learn skills from them..."

Wiz was carrying a backpack stuffed with... Well.

"Don't worry about them. I just decided not to leave any loose ends when I left. By which I mean...well, you see."

Wiz looked around. "Um... I'm not quite sure I do, considering you're on the ground, too, Kazuma."

"Oh, I'm just lying here, relaxing. It was me versus all of them, so practically speaking, I think this is a win for me."

"Get over yourself, Kazuma; you could hardly stand by the third opponent!"

"You looked like you were gonna start crying the second we attacked you, so we took it easy on you, that's all!"

Let the losers talk. In *numerical* terms, it was my victory.

Wiz, herself a former adventurer, seemed to catch on to what had happened as she listened to us. "I see... Adventurers do love to see one another off with a little violence, don't they? Well, don't mind if I do..."

"Wiz, if you 'saw me off' adventurer-style, I think I'd die even if you did hold back!" I forced my aching body upright and took the bag from Wiz. Just as I'd promised Vanir, once I'd gotten my money this morning, I'd bought a whole load of this stuff.

"All aboard! The carriage to Arcanletia will be leaving shortly!"

When the driver shouted, we shoved my cargo onto the carriage and then hopped aboard.

"You know, I've been wondering... What happened to your armor?" I asked.

Darkness, who wasn't wearing any armor but only had her great sword across her back, grinned and slapped the luggage she was clutching. "It's in here."

. . . .

"Look, we're leaving on a journey, here; you're supposed to be *wearing* it."

"I don't know what you're talking about. If I did that, my precious armor would get all scratched and dirty."

"I don't know what *you're* talking about!"

I guess Darkness had really taken to that armor I'd gotten her. She didn't look like she was going to let go of it anytime soon, so I ignored her and instead waved to the adventurers who were seeing us off. "Okay, I'll be right back with that idiot in tow!" I said.

"Yeah, see you soon! And take care of the Demon King while you're at it!"

"This is Aqua we're talking about. I'm sure she's lost in some ridiculous place! Make sure you check everywhere. She's probably stuck in a hole somewhere!"

"Hey, you better bring back souvenirs!"

"You can trust us to take care of the town. Heck, I've got a newborn kid and a beautiful wife here. I'd never let anything happen to 'em!"

Ah, trustworthy adventurers...

Wait... Did that last person just raise a super obvious death flag?

*   *   *

"Darkness, please put on your armor already! There is the problem of your Defense, plus, when you make such a show of cherishing your souvenir, it rather irks those of us who *did not get souvenirs!*"

"I'll put the armor on when we get somewhere dangerous—that ought to be enough! My Defense is more than high enough to handle the monsters around here!"

The two of them were having an inane argument. *These* were the two people with whom I was about to walk into the most dangerous place in this entire world? Crap! The various skills I'd just learned notwithstanding, I felt like my spirit was about to break.

"Hey, Kazuma! That sword you've got there, you had it made here in town, right? No magic or anything? Better take this one just to be safe!" Dust, who had a spear strapped across his back for some reason, tossed his sword up to me. Dang, that was actually pretty cool. Had he always been the type to say stuff like that? "It's got an enchantment on it, as far as it goes. It's not some legendary thing that can only be used by members of a certain class or whatever, so you should have no problem with it, Kazuma. But I want it back after you beat the Demon King!" Then he grinned. God, he actually sounded heroic.

Considering there were monsters out there that could be harmed only by enchanted weapons, I was awfully grateful to him for lending me this thing. Still, I didn't understand what had come over him. Was I going to have to change my opinion of him…?!

"Oh, I get it. On the off chance Kazuma just happens to defeat the Demon King with that thing, that weapon will be worth loads of cash. *The very blade the hero used!* you'll say. Hey, Kazuma, Dust probably just filched that thing off some dead adventurer in a dungeon, so you don't have to worry about giving it back to him!"

"Screw you, Rin! Don't get in the way of my brilliant get-rich-quick scheme!"

Ah. Never mind.

Truthfully, though, it was actually reassuring. Axel was populated almost exclusively by the obnoxious and the useless, but to my own surprise…I didn't hate it here. And I felt like if I could bring back Aqua, who'd sort of become the town mascot somewhere along the line, then maybe I could have a decent time even here in this dumb world.

I smiled a little to myself as I watched the street punk chase Rin away.

"Here we goooo!!"

Our carriage set out under the clear, blue sky.

We were headed off on our first and last serious adventure…!

5

"I didn't see Chris anywhere, even with all those adventurers. I would have liked to talk to her before we went off to fight the Demon King," Darkness said. "When she heard the king's goons were going to attack the capital, she said she'd be busy for a while, and I haven't seen her since then…"

"You know, you're right. I haven't seen her around. Eh, I guess I can sort of understand why she'd be busy, though." This was the big showdown at the capital between humanity and the Demon King's forces. Her *real* job was going to take over for a while.

"Why would you understand that, Kazuma?" Darkness said. "I'd love to press you for details, but… Well, both of you, have a look. What do you think?"

""Demon King's servant,"" we said flatly to Darkness, who was sitting in the rocking carriage, proudly wearing her new armor. She looked a little disappointed that Megumin and I had both had the exact same response.

"You look very much like a Dark Knight," Megumin said. "You would not seem out of place at the Demon King's side."

"You've got a big sword but no shield, so the black armor really accentuates the offensive impression," I added.

"Hrk…!" Darkness pouted, tracing her finger over the surface of the armor. The gear seemed to fit her every curve perfectly. The black metal gave off an eerie shimmer. The overall effect was less *cool* and more…beautiful. But sort of in the same way that a demon's blade or an enchanted sword was beautiful.

"By the way, Kazuma, did you hear? While you were in that dungeon, there was a bit of a commotion up here," Megumin said. I couldn't ignore that.

"That woman you captured, Serena, the general of the Demon King? She escaped," Darkness said.

"You're kidding."

What were the Axel police even doing?

"It seems Serena temporarily made a puppet of her guard and forced him to help her escape. He's now claiming that the Demon King's general is an exhibitionist."

"Yeah, the man she puppeted said he was shown something."

That would be Serena's panties. I was very sorry: I saw now that I had given Serena some truly destructive knowledge.

"They weren't able to spare anyone to chase her down, because everyone is needed to defend the town. The Guild put up a wanted poster asking anyone who saw Serena to capture her. There's a good chance she's heading back to the Demon King's castle, so since we are going the same way, we may well find her ourselves."

"Mm, and when we do, this time I'm going to make her pay. I have a score to settle with her," Darkness added.

Well, I guess if we caught her, we'd probably get a little reward for our trouble. If we happened to run across her on our trip, we could grab her—no need to go out of our way. She'd been reduced to Level 1; even without Aqua around, I figured we could handle her somehow.

I looked at the other carriages traveling behind us and said softly, "Huh, guess there aren't many customers…"

What with all the unsettling rumors of an imminent attack by the Demon King's forces, not many people were eager to travel right now. A few had fled to other towns, but by this point, most people who were going to leave had already done so. Other than the carriage we were in, the rest transported only merchant cargo, no passengers.

There were five carriages total. There was no one around except for the drivers and merchants and a handful of adventurer bodyguards riding in one of the vehicles. With so few carriages, even weaker monsters might not be intimidated enough to stay away. For us, hoping to catch up with Aqua, who had a good head start, traveling in such a small caravan was hardly ideal…

"By the way, Kazuma, how many skills did you ultimately acquire? Darkness and I simply gathered up everyone in town who was powerful or knew any useful abilities. We don't actually know what you learned."

Darkness breathed on her armor and polished it (*squeak, squeak*); Megumin seemed to take it as a challenge, because she started polishing her staff while she spoke to me.

"Well, magic-wise, I took Teleport and Intermediate Magic."

Megumin dropped her staff when I said that. "I-I-I-Intermediate Magic, is that so? W-well, at least you didn't take Advanced Magic." She was trying to act cool but couldn't hide a slight stutter. She bent down to pick up her staff…

"Yeah, Advanced Magic involves a lot of long chants and special instructions. And I guess you have to learn all the incantations to pick up the skill. I didn't have time for that. Wiz said she would teach me after we got back, though…"

Megumin went immediately from picking up the staff to attacking me with it. "Not satisfied with Intermediate Magic, you seek to learn even Advanced Magic! As if you didn't have me, an Arch-wizard, right here! Give me your Adventurer's Card, Kazuma! …Ah! If you use all your points, you could learn Explosion! I will acquire it for you and leave you with no points at all…!"

"H-hey, stop that! I left those points so I could get a *useful* skill like Advanced Magic! If you don't like it, learn some other magic yourself! Don't go messing with a person's Adventurer's Card without permission!"

"Says the man who did exactly that to my own card! Wait, what?! You've even learned Golem-Fashioning Magic and some healing spells?! Tell me. Do you seek to become a wizard, despite having less than one-tenth as much magic as I do?!"

"So you even learned healing magic. If Aqua ever finds out, she's going to cry that you took her job…"

We'd made the trip to Arcanletia before, but it went a lot faster this time. Last time, we'd had Darkness (as tough as she is) getting caught up in the "chicken races" of horny Dashing Hawkites and Aqua attracting undead to us. At this rate, though, it looked like we were going to reach Arcanletia by tomorrow morning.

"The bodyguards are going to stand guard all night. When we were doing that work, the campsite was beset by undead, but tonight I think things will be all right," Megumin said, obviously remembering the same things I was. She sounded a little nostalgic, though, and a little lonely. Probably reminded of the fact that we were missing someone.

"That's true," Darkness said. "With so few carriages and bodyguards, we would normally be ripe for attack by monsters, but this has actually been a really smooth, uneventful trip so far. It makes all the harrowing trips we've taken before seem like a dream." She sounded downright bored.

It was pitch-black by then, so we helped the merchants set up camp, then picked a place a little bit apart from everyone else and started a small bonfire. You needed one of those to keep away weak monsters. Although *someone* on our last trip had caused the undead to swarm us when we set up a campfire.

Like Darkness said, things had gone smoothly this time.

Too smoothly.

I wouldn't have expected it to be this easy, even without a certain someone with her terrible Luck along. I was just as happy nothing dangerous was happening. But I also found it sort of dull. Was that a sign that I'd been corrupted?

"Very well. It is time for you to tell me something that I've wanted to know for quite a while now," Megumin, leaning against our luggage, said out of the blue. Darkness was lying down by the cargo, too, clutching her armor, which was in a box resting on her belly; she looked up at the wide, starry night sky with sparkling eyes.

"Oh yeah," I said, "I never finished telling you what skills I learned." I spread my cape on the ground and sat down on it, tossing a couple of twigs into the fire.

"No, that is not what I meant. I expect to have plenty of opportunities during this trip to see what you've learned, so I'm not so concerned about that. Rather, I am referring to what Vanir said about you being from another world."

…………Oh. That.

I glanced over to find Darkness wasn't looking at the sky anymore but was studying me intently. In fact, both of them looked more solemn than usual.

"Oh, you don't have to take it so seriously. It's like…y'know. I'm not originally an inhabitant of this world. I come from somewhere else, somewhere far away. One day, I died in that other world. After that, a deity presented me with three choices and told me to pick. I could be reborn as a baby in my original world and have a do-over, or I could go to heaven. Or…I could go to another world."

It must have sounded ridiculous, but neither of them laughed or even looked surprised.

"I see. And I suppose Aqua is the deity you're referring to?"

"Yeah, exactly. She acted all high-and-mighty when we first met. I just thought I would make her life a little harder, so I dragged her along with me…"

*　　*　　*

Huh?

"Megumin, you never believed Aqua was a goddess. Whenever she claimed she was, you'd just be like, *That's nice* or *Oh, cool* or something…"

The two of them looked at each other and chuckled.

"It's true—I did not believe her at first. But there were too many strange things, too many questions. Coming back to life, for instance, is supposed to be the ultimate divine miracle, afforded only once, at most, to each person. But she resurrected you over and over. She can purify water with a single touch and is perfectly comfortable being underwater. And then… Well, there are no priests who can single-handedly face down a Lich or a greater demon."

……Fair enough.

Sheesh, so the two of them had figured it out ages ago? Actually, I was sort of impressed that hadn't changed their attitudes even a little after they'd realized they were dealing with a goddess. Unlike a Japanese person such as myself—raised on a steady diet of anime and manga in which gods and goddesses were treated as *moe* characters—I'd expected people from this world to be a bit more reverential.

"It doesn't matter what kind of being she is. Aqua is our cherished party member. The way she cries, the way she gets carried away, the way she screws up easily. And then there's the danger she drags us into, the way she loves to make everything difficult for you, Kazuma… It's so easy to laugh with her; she makes everything brighter just by being around. A cherished party member. That's right… I don't care *what* she is. Aqua is Aqua." Darkness was almost talking to herself, still cradling her box of armor and looking up at the stars.

Megumin smiled broadly at that, then sat up and looked squarely at me. "Kazuma, why is Aqua so set on defeating the Demon King? What will happen to her after she does it?"

She'll go back to the heavenly realm.

The words got stuck in my throat; they just wouldn't come out.

I was silent long enough that Megumin said, "Kazuma... After the Demon King is defeated, you won't go back to your original world or something, will you? You said once that you didn't intend to return to your country. So when this trip is over, we can all go home together, right? *With* you and Aqua." She sounded uneasy; in the starlight, her crimson eyes glowed eerily.

Darkness didn't say anything, just stared silently up at the sky.

"Hell, I couldn't go home, could I?" I said. "This world might suck, but somehow I've got friends here. Buddies, even. I've got a house and all the money I could ever need. Besides. In this world, I've got...you know..."

I glanced at them. Megumin started to smile. "I do not know. What is it that you have in this world?"

Darkness sat up, too. "Yeah, tell us, Kazuma. Don't act all embarrassed—spit it out. What is it? What do you have here?" They were both grinning at me.

Dammit, I shouldn't have let myself get swept up in the moment!

6

The next morning.

Maybe it was my fault for being dissatisfied with our smooth, trouble-free trip.

"A-a-adventurers! Monsters! There are monsters here! You're up!"

The driver's shout brought the bodyguards running from their carriage. In front of us was a horde of one of the very creatures I'd made mincemeat of in the dungeon a few days before: the man-eating devil, the ogre. They were gigantic, each over nine feet tall, and built like yakuza bruisers.

"What's a horde of ogres doing here?!" one of the adventurers shouted when they saw it. I didn't know how powerful ogres were—Vanir and Wiz had pinioned all the ones in the dungeon for me—but judging by that reaction, this was not a good situation.

The "horde" of ogres consisted of five monsters. Most of them had weapons; only the biggest one was barehanded. At that, I jumped out of my carriage, which was just behind the one carrying all the other adventurers.

"Megumin, Darkness!" I called. "Let's help out! If we're really going to take down the Demon King, we can't be intimidated by a few ogres!"

"I agree completely! For me, defeating this horde will take no time at all!"

"Oh, j-just a second! The barehanded guy is one thing, but even I need my armor if I'm going to take on ogres with weapons…"

I'd *told* her to put the damn armor on beforehand!

Ignoring Darkness, who was scrambling to get her armor out of its box, Megumin and I prepared to face off against the monsters.

We might be adventurers, but at this moment we were paying customers on a carriage ride. I felt bad, knowing that Megumin was all fired up, but I wanted to save our explosion. For this fight, we could restrict ourselves to playing a support role.

"Er gknew yer stinked of our brudders' blood!"

"Which erv yer diddit?! Gernta try'n hide, er yeh?!"

"Daz 'im in back! It's the wimpy-lookin' guy what stinks!"

The ogres sounded upset. It wasn't easy to make out what they were saying, but I thought I had the general idea.

Let's see: the weak-looking guy who killed their friends. That would be me.

Our bodyguards, all of whom had been hired in the beginner town, hadn't been expecting a bunch of ogres; they stood with their weapons drawn but looked distinctly unhappy.

"We'll handle the four short ones, noble leader. You take the big guy!"

"Wh-what, by myself?! Ugh, o-okay! Don't you die on me, you guys!" the person who appeared to be their leader said, and then he launched himself at the creatures.

The biggest ogre drew its sword and struck at the oncoming adventurer, cutting him down in a single stroke. The ogre barely glanced at the adventurer as he went flying aside; it just snorted and then headed for its target...!

"Megumin, Megumin! That guy just went *flying*!"

"Do not look away! Continue to make eye contact with them! In the natural world, the one who looks away first loses!" Megumin was glaring at them, her eyes shining crimson; beside her, I did my best to stare down the ogres, too.

"*'Ey, liddle man! Whodoya think yer insultin' here?! Graaahhh!*"

I immediately looked away.

"Why must you suddenly lose to them?! Now they think we are weak! The ogres are coming this way!"

"W-w-well, what was I supposed to do? They're terrifying!"

We couldn't exactly ask for help; the other bodyguards were all in the thick of a battle to defend the drivers and carriages. But I had awoken to my true potential as an overpowered protagonist. It wasn't time to panic yet!

"Watch closely, Megumin! I'm gonna show you the power unlocked by my awakening! Eat this! *Firebaaaaalll!*" I held my hands out toward the oncoming ogre and let off one of the magic spells I'd just learned!

"*Hoh...dat's hot. Nice liddle try dere...*"

The ogre, though, simply caught the ball of fire in his hand and crushed it out, then blew hurriedly on his palm.

I guess my fireball didn't merit any more than a "dat's hot."

"What the hell? Magic isn't working on this guy! Are ogres that strong?!"

"You simply do not have enough magical power! The Adventurer class doesn't get any bonuses to its skills, so with your wimpy magic, even a creature whose magic resistance is as low as an ogre's doesn't feel your attacks!" Megumin shouted at me, then started to perform the incantation for Explosion.

"Now iz my turn! Jez yoo n' mee hand-ta-hand, all manly like! Lez go!"

"Um, no thanks—I'm more the cerebral type!" I shouted back. I stood in front of Megumin, shielding her from the charging ogre. Then I pressed my hand to the ground.

It looked like I had to give up on attack magic. But I was always more the underhanded type anyway. For example…!

"Create Earth Golem!"

For example, using a golem in place of a wall. I could snipe from behind it to buy Megumin time to finish her incantation…

"Shit, why's it so small?! Why is it so *small*?! It hardly comes up to my waist! This isn't like my Fireball! I put plenty of MP into this one!"

"You don't have that much MP to begin with, Kazuma! It's all right—I've completed my incantation! And I don't mean that I'm constantly chanting explosion magic all day, every day, not at all! Here I go!"

I couldn't do anything with them! I'd finally learned all these skills, and I couldn't do a damn thing with them! Here I thought I was going to get to charge in all *Warriors*-like, but boy, was I wrong!

I grabbed my bow and decided to make use of a skill I was already well acquainted with: Deadeye. Megumin might be done with her chant, but you couldn't be too careful!

"Arrrrghhh! Damn! They're gonna destroy us!" one of the bodyguards shouted as I was getting ready. Megumin twitched, glanced in their direction, and then:

"Explooooosion!!"

She dropped an explosion directly onto the ogres who were going for the drivers. She'd probably done her best to put the epicenter up in the air so that the other adventurers didn't get caught in the blast, but many were still thrown to the ground and knocked unconscious by the sheer force of it. Still, it was better than the alternative. Specifically, the alternative in which we would all have been dead.

We still had a problem, though…

"D-damn it! Darkness, Darkness! Aren't you ready yet?!"

I had Megumin, collapsed from using up all her MP, on my back, and I was firing arrows at the ogre. It didn't matter that I was shooting him from point-blank range; he just held his hands in front of his face and blocked every shot.

"Ta take downna bigger opponent! Y'always gofer th' eyezz! Combat basicz!"

"This is why I hate intelligent monsters! Go forth, golem! Your name is—"

But before I could name my tiny golem (whom I'd hoped to use as a shield), it was crushed underfoot.

"Buggerroff, ya liddle—"

"That thing was *no* damn help!"

The ogre was focused squarely on me at the moment. Hoping to save Megumin from being the target of any attacks, I took the instant while he was crushing my golem to run like my life depended on it. The ogre leaped, punched at me, and—

"Emergency Evade!"

"…?!"

I pirouetted neatly out of the way of an attack from an advanced monster, the sort of thing I would never normally have been able to dodge. It was an auto-evade ability taught to me by a monk—that is, a cleric who fights with their bare hands. It gave you a very high chance of dodging an enemy's attack: the perfect thing for me.

The ogre, shocked to miss its swing, turned back to me. I drew out the enchanted sword Dust had lent me, its polished blade catching the sunlight with a gentle glow.

Sure, now I had my sword out, but that didn't mean I had to go toe to toe with it. I wasn't alone, after all. All I had to do was buy time.

With my newly increased level, I should be able to take one good attack from an ogre and keep on—

"Run away, right now!" Megumin shouted when she saw me getting ready to meet my opponent. "An ogre's attacks can leave even veteran adventurers at death's door! For a weakling like you, they'd be critical!"

If I got seriously injured while Aqua wasn't here, I wouldn't get any second chances.

The ogre was rushing at me with its arms spread wide, as if to indicate it wasn't going to let me dodge the next one.

"O-okay! Okay! We can talk! We can talk like civilized people. Maybe we can come to an understanding…"

"You cover yerself inna stink 'a my brudders' blood and then you wanna TALK?!" With an ogre who looked like a yakuza enforcer facing me down, I thought I might just pee my pants.

"K-Kazumaaaa!" Megumin shouted.

As for me, I cried, "Ahhhh! If I'd known things were going to turn out like this, I would have just done it with you yesterday instead of acting all coool! I don't wanna die a virgiiiiiin!"

"Th-this man! Even at a moment like this—!"

The ogre was closing in on me (and the wish I'd let slip at the moment of my death).

But suddenly, something hard and pitch-black slammed the ogre away.

Who or what had appeared at my moment of greatest need? Of course, it was…

"Took you long enough! This is why I said you should just keep the armor on!"

"Y-yeah, but then I was worried it would start to smell sweaty…!"

…Darkness, who'd been in the carriage getting her armor on until that exact moment, was blushing and making excuses. She drew her great sword and turned to face the ogre, which she'd shoved out of the way with a tackle. An ogre's attacks might be terrifying, but I was willing to bet Darkness could hold out against one even in a long fight. While she was keeping it busy, if I could go around and wake up the other adventurers...

"I'm gonna kill you!" Darkness cried (most unladylike) before I could get the suggestion out of my mouth. She started swinging wildly at the ogre with her sword.

"You don't have to bother attacking it, Darkness, just buy us time until I can wake up the other—" I stopped mid-sentence. Something about Darkness looked strange.

"Kazuma, is it just me, or does Darkness not seem like her usual self? She isn't normally so aggressive."

Darkness, breathing hard, was gleefully chasing the ogre around. The masochist Crusader we knew so well was gone; even when the ogre attacked her, she simply absorbed the hits with her armor, shrugged them off, and went back after it...

"Ha-ha-ha-ha-ha! Bwa-ha-ha-ha-ha-ha-ha-ha!"

"Hey, Darkness, that laugh is starting to sound like a certain demon's! It's got to be the armor! That must be what's doing it!"

The pitch-black armor Darkness was wearing didn't just reflect the sunlight; it seemed to glow with its own weird illumination. I didn't know whether it was blessed or cursed, but whatever power it was radiating, Darkness was obviously high on it.

Fine, we could get the armor off her later... What mattered right then was the ogre!

"Yanno howta fight, missie! And ripped abs, too—wanna join m' gang?"

Darkness, short-tempered as ever, rose to the bait immediately. "That's it! I'm gonna chop you into a million pieces!" This was starting to look dangerous, so I abandoned the idea of waking up the other adventurers and decided to focus on helping Darkness. Taking pot shots with my arrows was all well and good, but this situation called for a little magic...!

"Try this on for size! *Flash!*"

"*Ahhhhhh?!*"

My illumination magic produced an intense light with zero casting time. It blinded the ogre facing off with Darkness, and—

"Gaaah! My eyes! My eyeeeees!"

"Wh-what do you think you are doing?! What good are you if you blind yourself with your own magic?!"

I'd been looking directly into the light, and it damn near blinded me. Shit! Betrayed by the skill I just learned! I should have actually practiced a little, instead of assuming I'd make an amazing awakening debut in front of everyone!

"*Grah! Now yeh've dunnit, yeh—!*"

As I writhed on the ground waiting for my sight to come back, I heard the ogre's voice. Darkness must have finished off the blinded creature.

"Kazuma, are you a complete idiot or a total genius?" I still had my eyes closed as Megumin, sounding exasperated, pulled me to my feet.

"A-all this trouble is because of *you*, you runaway! Just wait till I find youuu!!" I howled at Aqua—wherever she was and whatever she was doing.

We'd spent a little less than an hour in a rocking carriage on the way to Arcanletia.

"Um, Cecily, I'm getting pretty tired of this," I muttered.

"I feel the same way, Lady Aqua. Perhaps we should go home soon, then?" Cecily replied immediately.

"Normally, I would definitely say we should, but we can't. After all, if we go home now, no one will save the people suffering under the Demon King." For a second there, I'd almost caved and decided to turn around.

"That's Lady Aqua for you. But I certainly understand being tired of traveling by carriage. Perhaps we should ask the driver if we could take a break soon?"

"No, Cecily, we've hardly left Axel. We were late leaving, and now I'm afraid Kazuma is going to catch up with me."

Cecily had shown me the way to the carriage depot, but then she'd wanted to go back to the Axis church to get a bunch of baggage, so we ended up missing the first carriage in the morning.

"I'm very sorry, Lady Aqua. It just takes a good woman a while to get ready."

"You're right—it's not your fault. There are *only* good women in the Axis Church, after all."

Maybe I would have to start deliberately taking extra time to get ready to leave from now on, just to make sure I was being a "good woman."

"I have to say, though, this carriage seems to be going awfully slowly," I remarked. "The last time we all went to Arcanletia together, I didn't have time to enjoy the scenery like this."

Cecily smiled as she looked out at the landscape rolling past. "This is a special tourist carriage that takes its time so you can enjoy the view. Oh, look over there, Lady Aqua! It's a group of Blue Crabs. They travel long distances protected from enemies and the desiccating effects of the sun by their hard shells. It's too early for egg-laying season, so they must be going to fight over territory."

"You sure know your crabs, Cecily. Hang on… Did you say this is a special tourist carriage? But I want to get to the Demon King's castle as fast as possible!" Those Blue Crabs were interesting, but somehow, I felt like this wasn't the time.

"Lady Aqua, there's a reason I chose this carriage. It's not a cheap one, and that's because they hire lots of guards to protect the tourists. If anything were to happen to an Arch-priest like you, Lady Aqua, it would be a loss for the entire world. You know they say 'slow and steady wins the race,' right? Well, let's take it slow and steady here."

"I see; having strong bodyguards along is definitely a plus. Slow and steady it is, then." What a smart woman Cecily was.

"Besides, the Axis Church will cover the expenses, so I figured, why *not* take an expensive ride?"

"That's a very good idea. Expensive is wonderful! And it doesn't make your butt sore!"

That was when it happened.

"Passengers, please be aware, the carriage is stopping! Some ogres have been spotted, presumably hunting the Blue Crabs! We'll be halting until they pass through!"

I looked up at the driver's voice to see several ogres chasing after the crabs. "Cecily, don't ogres usually eat people?"

"I'm sure even they feel like crab from time to time, Lady Aqua."

....

"You know, *I* feel like crab right about now."

"What a coincidence, Lady Aqua. I'd love to eat some crab, too. And there are such fresh ones walking right in front of us."

We glanced at the driver, a middle-aged man who smiled a little and shrugged at us. "Look at the size of that group. I don't suppose the ogres would be upset if you plucked one or two from the edge of the crowd. We've got some very capable guards we hired right in the next carriage. Why not go ahead and see if you can get your hands on some crabs?"

His suggestion gave me an even better idea. "We don't even have to go near them. We can get the crabs to come to us!"

"Lady Aqua, I know it may not be my place, but perhaps I could ask what you're planning to do next?"

I started preparing my spells as I replied, "I'm just going to get their attention."

"I'm afraid that doesn't tell me much, Lady Aqua. My priest's intuition gives me a bad feeling about this pattern, though..."

I let loose with my magic before she could go any further. "It's been a while since I used this! We're in for a huge catch of crab today! *False Fire!*"

"Not a *huge* catch!" Cecily cried.

The crabs came scuttling toward the blue flames I unleashed, followed by the ogres...

"Waaaaahhh! I haven't done *this* in a while, either! Kazumaaaaa!"

"I don't hate how you're this way, Lady Aquaaaaaa!"

1

"Just stop causing so much trouble already! Take it *off*! Or do you want me to tear it off you?! Stop fighting me!"

"N-no, don't! I...I can't believe this...! What's gotten into you, Kazuma? What sudden impulse...causes you to lust after my body like a wild animal...?!"

What an idiot!

"I mean take off that stupid armor! Why do you always, always go charging into the enemy formation?! It's cursed! I'm sure that armor has a curse on it!"

"It's not cursed! A cursed item can't be removed once it's equipped and continues to cause catastrophe for the wearer until they die. I'm able to take this armor off, so that weird excitement that comes over me in battle must be a blessing, not a curse!"

"So you admit you get weirdly excited in battle! That'll make things easy. I don't care if it's a curse or a blessing or what, just take it off already! C-come on—stop fighting me! I'll buy you the very best armor in town, just get this thing off!"

After leaving Axel, we and the other adventurer bodyguards had been involved in a number of other fights with monsters, until we finally made it to Arcanletia, but...

"No way! You gave this to me as a gift; you can't take it back! It's the very first armor anyone's ever given me, and it's special Crusader equipment with powerful enchantments to boot! I'm going to hand this down as an heirloom in the Dustiness family. I've made up my mind. Until we defeat the Demon King, I'm not taking this armor off except for when I sleep and when I bathe."

"Why'd you have to get so stubborn all of a sudden?! I can't use any of my offensive magic because you keep winding up right in the middle of it! Do you know how much suffering you've caused on this trip?! The adventurers who are *supposed* to be guarding us pretty much end up in tears every time!"

We were standing in the road in Arcanletia, and I was arguing with Darkness, who steadfastly refused to take off the armor I'd given her. Whatever it was, it clearly had some weird side effects. It appeared to banish fear from the wearer's heart and cause courage to well up within them. Probably would have been a huge blessing for a normal Crusader, but with *our* Crusader, it just meant more trouble.

The upshot of this side effect was that when a battle started, Darkness went charging straight at the monsters, regardless of what anyone else said.

I'd forgotten that Wiz had picked out this armor. I knew her sense of judgment, and I should have been perfectly well aware of what that implied...

It was then that Megumin, who had been observing the argument closely, spoke. "Perhaps we should give up, Kazuma. The side effects are no doubt strange, but this armor is certainly a good thing. It may indeed be legendary-tier equipment. With this on, she might even survive one of my explosions."

"What are you saying?! That you would do it? Are you saying you would drop an explosion on a bunch of monsters even if Darkness was in there with them?!"

Darkness met this obnoxious pronouncement with folded arms and a nod. "I wouldn't mind in the least. The last time one of Megumin's explosions hit me, I lost consciousness. But this time I'll pull through."

"A good point. This journey might be the perfect time to settle once and for all which is greater: my magic or Darkness's durability."

"Save it for when we have Aqua back or when we return to Axel! In fact, just stop already! If you won't take that armor off, I really will tear it off you!" I said, and then I stuck my hand out toward Darkness, assuming the Steal position...!

"Go ahead, try it."

"Huh?" I said dumbly.

Darkness, her arms still folded, responded, "I said, try it. I couldn't care less."

I was shocked she would say something so stupid right out in public.

"Wh-what's wrong with you? This is Steal we're talking about. Right out in public. You saying you want a humiliation game out here in front of everybody?"

"At this moment, I can't be broken with such talk! Besides, I'm the only one who's never experienced your Steal. That might have been enough to make me back down before, but with the blessing of this armor filling me with courage, I fear nothing now. So go ahead and do it! I know you always get cold feet at the crucial moment. If you think you can tear this off me 'out here in front of everybody,' then just you try!"

"Y-you pervert! Why're you so aggressive?! Are you even listening to yourself? I knew there was something wrong with that armor! Fine, I can't do it—I admit it! So just back off!"

The pervert (her lewdness focused in an ever more awful direction by the armor) was bearing down on me.

"This is quite odd... We're making all this commotion, and yet, no one has come to gawk. I'm sure most of the population of this city is made up of Axis followers. And they are always full of curiosity, love fights and trouble, adore chaotic situations, and will never fail to get in on the action in the hopes of doing even more damage. Standing by the roadside and shouting about how Darkness may have her armor torn off should bring them running."

"I sure get tired of the trouble they cause, but you know what?

You're right. The last time we were here, you couldn't keep the evangelists away with a stick. What's going on?" When I looked around, I realized that, in fact, there was hardly anyone else on the street at all. It was awfully quiet…

"Doesn't it seem like there aren't many people around for such a big town? What's going on here? Did something happen?" Darkness surveyed the land as well, then tilted her head in curiosity.

It was Megumin who suggested, "Perhaps we can ask about what has happened as we continue our journey. From this point, we have to decide whether to take a carriage or to walk, so we better get started arranging our transportation."

2

"Welcome, welcome! What would you like? We have a limited-time daily lunch special that comes with something sweet. If you want my recommendation, that's it. Incidentally, this shop offers a thirty percent discount for Axis followers. Take one of these if you're interested!" The waitress smiled broadly and handed us menus along with sheets of paper. The papers were, naturally, professions of faith in the Axis Church.

…Ah, yes. Arcanletia was like that. We had come to the restaurant in hopes of getting information and lunch at the same time, but we were immediately receiving our baptism in the ways of this city.

"Um… Okay, I'll have the lunch special."

"Certainly! And for you, Miss?"

"A Neroid and a sandwich, please."

"Of course!" The waitress continued to beam as she took Megumin's and my orders.

Then Darkness opened the menu. "Let's see. I'll have—"

"—dirt shoved in your stupid face, I hope," the waitress spat, her smile never slipping. Then she went into the kitchen.

"……" Darkness sat there with her menu open, shaking, her face flushing.

"Geez," I said, "hide your Eris pendant when we come to this city."

"I... I will not..."

Darkness had made sure the pendant was clearly visible from the moment we arrived in Arcanletia; I guess our last visit had given her a taste for the sort of treatment she received while she was wearing it here.

"Still, this place does seem awfully quiet for lunchtime. Normally, this town is always bustling with freaks and weirdos," Megumin, *a member of the Crimson Magic Clan*, said of the Axis Church.

It was true, though, that everything seemed like a lot less trouble than the last time we had been here. Back then, we'd been the object of depressing invitations just walking down the street...

"The Axis followers of this town have gone, under the command of Lord Zesta, highest leader in the Axis Church, to clear the monsters from the path to the Demon King's castle," declared a woman standing proudly in front of the Axis church building. A follower herself, she bore a blue chest plate and carried a mace in one hand and a silver shield in the other.

We'd come to the church after lunch, figuring it was the best place to get information. With Darkness in the middle of it all at the restaurant, we'd lost the opportunity to ask them for any tips.

"So Axis followers actually do something for the world's benefit every once in a while," Darkness observed.

"Please stop viewing us Axis followers as if we live only to cause trouble to others. All nasty rumors about the Axis Church are started by heartless, evil Eris followers." The woman sounded downright grief-stricken as she stood protectively in front of the church building.

"Say, why aren't you with the others?"

"With most of the Axis followers out of town, the bill for having done exactly as we liked every day is coming due. The city's various minority groups, starting with the female clerics of Eris, are coming to do mischief to our church."

"So you *do* know that you run roughshod over this town! You going to be all right by yourself?" I was just a little worried for the woman, who looked familiar to me.

"I'll be fine. I have this big, hard, thick mace that I'll pound into any heretics who may accost me."

"S-stop that! This is why people speak poorly about the Axis Church! By the way... Have you seen an Arch-priest named Aqua around here? She's a companion of mine. We're trying to get some information, but none of the shops in this town will hear us out."

The woman smiled brightly when she heard the name *Aqua*. "She was here! Yes, Lady Aqua was here! She flinched as she came into town, saying, 'You're...not mad that I purified the mainspring?' My, but she was adorable! In fact, it was her words that sent all the city's Axis followers out on the road! Ahhh, how I wish I could have joined that monster hunt...! Unfortunately, I lost the game of rock-paper-scissors to see who would stay behind."

She scuffed her feet, kicking a nearby stone. She had been talking fast, obviously excited. The stone jumped up and smacked Darkness in the shin guard, but the woman didn't appear to mean any harm.

"They're hunting monsters on Aqua's orders? What's that about? I'd like to hear a little more about that."

"Lady Aqua said, 'O Axis followers, who walk every day upon my pure and righteous path. So that travelers and stuff may move safely and quickly along the road between here and the Demon King's castle, I request that you, strong and indomitable and cool as you are, exterminate all the monsters that threaten that path. Do so, and on the day that the Demon King is defeated, Lady Aqua, who was merely passing through this world, might just show up here for a visit and be all, *I was a goddess all along!* She may indeed give compliments and gratitude to each one of you.'"

The woman recited this entire speech in rapture, totally oblivious to the tears forming in Darkness's eyes when the stone had hit her armor.

Something felt off here, but I wasn't quite sure what it was. Wait, that was it: This lady's reaction to Aqua was really weird. Yeah, almost like...

"Like all you Axis followers already know who Aqua really is..."

The words sort of slipped out. It was most obvious with Cecily, the Axis priest who'd been sent to Axel.

"But of course we do. Our unclouded vision has no blind spots, you know?"

She couldn't be serious.

"But you guys accused Aqua of being a fake! You tried to stone her…"

"That was the doing of Eris followers in Axis believers' clothing. I don't remember being any part of it myself."

Man, she sure could lie with a straight face.

But forget about that. Why was Aqua trying to make the road safer? Could it possibly be that she'd expected us to come after her? Sheesh, she really was just like a kid who'd run away but secretly wanted to be found. Instead of going to all this trouble, she could have just slowed down a little.

Grrr, just how much of a headache did she mean to make for me…?!

"Erm, was Aqua alone? She didn't happen to be accompanied by a nasty hunk with a magic sword or a sad-looking Crimson Magicker, did she?"

"Ah yes, I did see people fitting that description. When I went to the city gate to see Lady Aqua off, the hunk with the expensive-looking sword got into a very fancy carriage, as if he was specifically rubbing my nose in it after I lost all my money trying to play the market. He somehow remained unmoved by even my most powerful come-hither glance."

She was starting to let her trash-fire side show.

But anyway, that meant Mitsurugi and Yunyun had managed to link up with Aqua. That made me feel a little better.

"Okay, so she's got protection… Oh, I meant to ask. Is there a place around here where we can rent a carriage? I don't care if it's a little pricey; we just need something that can go fast…"

"I believe the horses kept by this very church are the fastest in the city… But you, the Eris follower, you can go crawling on all fours like the dog you are. It's only fitting for an evil follower of Eris like you to— Hey! What are you doing, you damnable heretic?!"

Darkness must have finally hit her breaking point, because she was suddenly involved in a wrestling match with the woman.

Meanwhile, I held out a fistful of eris bills to the impoverished believer and said, "Sorry, but could we borrow those horses? If money is the issue..."

"The Goddess Aqua's blessings on you!"

3

We stayed one night at the Axis church so Megumin could recover her MP; then we set out by carriage to go after Aqua. Maybe the Axis monster-extermination campaign was working, because even though the roadway looked long abandoned, travel was perfectly smooth.

Well, "smooth"...

"Hey, Darkness, it's terrific that we're making great time at all, but don't you think we're going a *little* fast? We can afford to slow down just a tad. The Axis followers obviously did good work, but there's no way they uprooted all the monsters. What if an enemy comes jumping out and spooks the horses?"

Darkness, sitting in the driver's seat with the reins in her hands, didn't respond.

When you were traveling with only a few people, it was best to go with the smallest carriage available. And two people could ride in a two-horse vehicle. So Darkness was in the driver's seat, while Megumin and I sat behind her.

"Um, Darkness...? I agree that we seem to be truly flying. I sympathize with your concern for Aqua, but if you go too fast, won't you tire out the horses?" Megumin sounded just as worried as I was about our pace.

"........." Darkness, though, didn't respond, and she didn't slow down.

Starting to feel uneasy, I tried again. "Hey, are you listening? We said you're going too fast. We need to slow down a little..."

Finally, Darkness turned to me, and I could see tears in her eyes. "The horses... They won't do what I tell them..."

""......................"" Now it was Megumin's and my turn to fall silent.

"I've heard about this," Darkness went on. "They say that in Arcanletia, even the horses are brainwashed by the Axis Church. They won't listen to anyone but an Axis follower..."

"You've got to stop them!"

"Oh! Kazuma, look! There's a profession of faith in the Axis Church tucked in the corner of the carriage! We've been had! That believer trapped us!"

Sitting there in the runaway carriage, I was reminded just how crazy Axis Church followers could be.

"Arrrrgh, damn it all! We should have destroyed the Axis Church before we bothered about the Demon King's army!"

"K-Kazuma! I think you, as our representative, ought to sign the paper so that..."

"H-hey, listen to me! How about this? If you do what we ask, I'll give you some nice fresh vegetables later! So fresh they jump right off the plate!" Darkness was trying to reason with the horses; I could only hold my head in my hands and scream.

Megumin had picked up the profession of faith but lost her balance in the careering carriage. And then Darkness shouted: "Oh no, there's someone up ahead! Kazuma, what do we do? We're going to run those people over!"

Despite the rattling carriage, I somehow managed to get my balance well enough to look down the road, and there was indeed a crowd of people ahead of us. And not just a couple of them, either! At this rate...!

Then Megumin said, "Let us run them over."

....

"I do not care. Darkness, simply drive straight through them."

"M-Megumin?!" Darkness said, looking at Megumin with a pained expression, and that was when, belatedly, I realized who the silhouettes were.

"I do not care," Megumin insisted. "In fact, I hope you will run over as many of them as possible! Standing at the head of that group is—!"

The crowd seemed to have noticed the oncoming carriage, because the figures scattered. But one man continued standing smack in the middle of the road. He saw Megumin in the carriage and shouted something.

It was a white-haired old guy dressed in cleric's robes and a metal breastplate. He was clearly waving at us.

"Well, well, Miss Megumin! It's been so long—do you remember me? It's me, the most important person in the Axis Church—"

The carriage went plowing right over the most important person in the Axis Church.

4

"*Heal*! *Heal*! How's that? Any better?"

Granted, our carriage had been rampaging because of an Axis follower, but even so, I felt compelled to use my newly acquired Heal skill on the person we had just run over.

"Yes, that's much better. Goodness, I could have done it myself. But a youngster's Heal is quite nice! Not only my flesh, but my soul has been rejuvenated!"

"That's Lord 'Anything Goes' Zesta for you! He's a diehard!"

"You know what he always says: 'I'll try anything once, even an orc!' You go! Lord Zesta, you go and go and go!"

Zesta: the entire time I had been casting Heal on him, he'd said only the most awful things. So this guy was the Church's head honcho, huh?

"It's been such a long time, Miss Megumin. I never imagined our reunion would be prefaced with such a brutal greeting, though. I'm afraid the only ways you could apologize for this would be to join the Axis Church or to go steady with me."

"For the record, it was the rampaging horses we borrowed from *your* church that caused us to run you over, sir. Please don't do anything...*strange* to them." Megumin glowered at the old fart with his bizarre pronouncements, then heaved a sigh.

The old guy turned to me. "I've heard a great deal about you, Master Kazuma! You're welcome to call me Zesta—no need for a title—but you can also feel free to call me Papa, Darling, or Daddy. Whatever you like."

"Megumin, a word of advice. You should be more careful about the company you keep."

"It was not my choice to become acquainted with these people! Speaking of advice, Kazuma, I think you should heed your own. You wouldn't want to be corrupted by this lot, would you?"

At that, I looked around again. The crowd was full of men and women, up to and including the elderly; everybody was dressed in different outfits so that at first glance, it wasn't obvious what sort of a group it was. But they all had one thing in common. Namely...

"Hey, Big Bro, you look like a really cool guy! I can call you 'Big Bro,' can't I?"

"Stop that! True, he's quite handsome and seems like an outstanding person, but I don't know about calling someone who's not an Axis follower 'Bro'... I know you want a big brother to be friends with you, but pick one from the Church, okay? What a shame; he is *so* handsome..."

"Awww, okay... Hey, Big Bro, don't you like the Axis Church?" The little girl looked at me anxiously.

I don't not *like it.*

I managed to swallow the words before they got out.

Growing impatient with my lack of an answer, the little girl and the woman I assumed was her mother reached out and touched hands with another believer. The person they switched off with was a cutie-pie wearing a frilly gothic-Lolita dress, who looked up at me pleadingly. "Um... May I...call you Elder Brother?"

"Like hell you can! I hear that bass in your voice! You're a man, aren't you?! First Zesta, now you! Will the Axis Church take *anyone*?!"

"I'm not *anyone*! I'm like Lord Zesta! Any and all are welcome, both in the Church and in—"

"Stop, shut up, just go away! I've got all the fashionable archetypes I need with my hard-masochist Crusader!"

"Huh?!" Darkness pointed to herself, apparently disagreeing with my characterization; meanwhile, I chased Goth-Loli Boy away.

I couldn't believe this. It was exhausting talking to these people. But there was someone here who looked even more exhausted than we were.

Namely…

"Looks like you really had a rough time of it. Man, you've lost weight," I said.

"Aw, shaddup… Pfah, what are you even doing here? The only thing around is a tiny village that serves as a forward base against the Demon King's army. Ugh, I feel sick…! First I get caught up with this bunch of goons, and now I run into the one guy in the whole world I least want to see!"

The speaker was a priest, who kicked a rock near her foot angrily as she spoke.

Serena: escapee from the Axel police station, worshipper of a dark goddess, murderer of me, and general of the Demon King. For some reason, she was with these Axis followers and looking very frustrated by it. I guess the "priest" disguise had gotten her swept up in the monster hunt.

As Darkness continued to mope from being called an "archetype" and Megumin got ready to fight, her temple twitching, the Axis followers (unable to read a room) started sexually harassing Serena.

"Bah! Where do you get off, having such a sexy body?! Where are you from and what religion do you follow? You'd better tell us!"

"Yeah, yeah—we'll go pay 'em a little visit, so make with the spittin' it out!"

"Hey! If you come around behind her, you can see her bra strap, clear as day! With boobs this big, maybe she really *doesn't* have anything to do with the Eris Church…?!"

"No, hold on—a paper has been submitted to our academy arguing that religion and bust growth might not be so closely related after all. To give us some more data for the resolution of that debate, we'll need you to tell us what religion you are! Specifically, which church in which town you hail from, and at what time of day we should show up to meet the clergy! I promise, we aren't intending to gleefully charge over there to sexually harass them in the name of holy war, so please, don't worry on that account!"

"……Y-you all don't know when to quit, do you…?"

I turned toward Serena, who was obviously nearing her limit, and said, "Actually, this is perfect timing, meeting you here. There were some questions I wanted to ask you. It does kind of tick me off the way you killed me, but if you tell me what I want to know, I might just pretend I didn't see you here."

Serena gave me the same kind of look you might give the dirt under your shoe and: *"Pfah!"*

"""""""Ahhh!"""""""

She spat on the ground as if to say that was her answer. The Axis followers cried out; I guess they objected to her prickly attitude.

"Heh. Think before you speak, kid. Why would I answer your questions? What, you going to compensate me somehow, again? Hell, I don't even want you for a puppet anym— Hey, what are you all doing?! S-stop that! Why are you digging up the ground I spat on?!"

That's what was happening: A crowd of Axis believers was digging up the dirt Serena's spit had landed on and were fighting over it. Man, these guys were on a different level from me. I couldn't keep up.

I didn't know (and didn't want to know) what they wanted to do with it, but Zesta won the fight for the dirt and triumphantly put it in a bottle, which he tucked into his robes as if it were a priceless treasure.

"Phew… My apologies, young lady, that my fellow believers should show you such an uncouth side of themselves."

"You're one to talk! Throw that stuff away; it's so creepy! Anyway, what are you guys? You've been abusing me to your hearts' content all this time, but not one of you seems to think you owe me anything—what's with that?! All this sexual harassment, you ought to at least feel a little gratitude!"

Zesta threw up his hands theatrically. "Gratitude?! Oh, we feel gratitude indeed, to our goddess! Ah yes, this blessed day is all thanks to our devout lifestyles and unyielding faith…! Ah, how grateful we are…!" He bowed his head deeply in Serena's direction as he spoke.

"I don't understand these people. They're all completely insane! Arrrgh, I feel like I don't understand *anything* anymore! And, Kazuma, what are you doing here anyway? I was sure I cast Instant Death on— Hey, you old fart! Don't pretend to bow to me just to catch a glimpse of my panties! Quit it already or I'll kill you!"

It didn't matter how much Serena howled and threatened; nothing deterred the Axis followers.

"You remember a priest called Aqua, right? She might not have much else going for her, but she's a damn good priest. She brought me back with resurrection magic. So, about those questions I wanted to ask you…"

I had been trying to offer an explanation, but Serena reached for the mace she kept at the small of her back. "Like I said before, why would I answer any questions of yours? Want to try to force it out of me? My level might have dropped, but I'm still the equal of everyone here. Besides, it doesn't look like that priest friend of yours is around to resurrect you right now. So what do you think? Still want to do it?"

Serena had a blessing from the goddess of revenge. She smirked, knowing that as long as she had that, I couldn't do anything to her. She might be a piece of trash, but she was still a general of the Demon King; even with her level at rock bottom, she had confidence to spare.

Darkness was clenching her fists so hard, I could hear it, and Megumin's eyes were blazing crimson when Serena said:

*　　*　　*

"Aqua, is that what you said her name was? I should have killed her first, not you. Huh, that was my mistake…"

The air went cold.

The Axis followers who had moved around behind Serena, trying to get a look at her bra strap.

The Axis kids who had been busily throwing stones at the Eris follower, Darkness.

The Axis women who had been sleepily watching the whole affair, just killing time.

And last but not least…

"*What* did you just say?"

Zesta asked as he crawled on the ground, trying to somehow get a look at Serena's panties. Mr. Most Important Person in the Axis Church had lost all expression on his face; his voice was quiet, and as he stood up, he didn't even bother to brush the dirt from his knees.

"What do you mean, what?" Serena, who hadn't noticed the changed atmosphere, stopped pointing her mace at me and rested it across her shoulder. "I said I should have killed that bumbling Aqua girl. So what's *your* answer, Kazuma? My patience has just about run out. You want to live, you're gonna have to beg. You know what a dangerous opponent I am. But I know what a pain in the ass *you* are, so if you throw yourself on the ground, I'd probably let you go, eh? Ah, but…" She smirked as if she was completely in control of the situation. "…this lot, not so much. I guess they're friends of yours, but they've harassed me one time too many. We're close enough to the Demon King's territory that no heroic knights are gonna come and save you, either. So how about it?" Bursting with confidence, she switched her mace to her other shoulder, *thump*.

"Master Kazuma. You seem to know who this young lady is.

Perhaps you could introduce me," Zesta said. The airheaded attitude was gone; his voice was completely flat, no intonation, no emotion.

I glanced at Serena as if to ask whether I could tell them who she really was.

"Go ahead, introduce me," she said. "Not like they're gonna leave this place alive anyway. They might as well die lamenting having offended me."

Wow, she was almost as bad at reading a crowd as Aqua was.

I gestured at Serena and said, "This is Serena. Dark Priest, worshipper of the dark goddess Regina, and the one who ultimately hurt Aqua so badly that she decided to leave town." Then I waved at the Axis followers, who had gone deadly silent, all of them looking grim. "And these are those Axis followers you hear so many bad things about, all from Arcanletia, along with Zesta, the most important person in the Axis Church."

When I'd finished my introduction, there was a *wumph*.

I looked toward the sound. Serena was pale-faced, shivering, and drenched in sweat. She'd dropped her mace.

5

We were on a small road, not much used these days, that led to the Demon King's castle. Typically you wouldn't see anyone there; you'd hear only the insects and the birds. But today…

"""*Get a rope! Tie her up!!*"""
"Sttttttttttooooooooooooooooooooopppppppppppppppppp!!"

The first chorus of voices belonged to the enraged female Axis killers—er, I mean, followers—while the second belonged to Serena, tears streaking down her cheeks as she hung from the tree where they'd strung her up. It was a pretty tall tree, and Serena's face was covered with tears and snot and contorted in terror.

"I-I-I'b breally zorry! Please forgib me! I didn't know! I d-d-d-didn't, I didn't know that lady was your goddess!"

"What was that? *'That lady'*? You dare refer to our glorious deity as *'that lady'*?"

"Heek! S-sorry, I'm sorry!"

The women got angrier and angrier with every word that came out of Serena's mouth. The way they pulled on the rope, which was slung over the branches of the tall tree, they could have stood proud among the ranks of religious fanatics anywhere at any time in history.

After she dropped her mace, Serena had tried, trembling, to run away, but they'd caught her in short order. Then they'd tied her up like a bagworm, and now it looked like the Axis women were going to put her to death…

"Uh, hey. Sorry, but I'd like to ask her a few questions," I said, keeping a distance between myself and the murderous Axis believers. "Think you could give me a hand? It'll help Aqua."

Serena twisted from her perch, trying to cling to me. "K-Kazuma! H…! Help me! I'll tell you whatever you want to know—just save me! We're friends, aren't we?! We were fellow worshippers of Regina for a while there! I let you do whatever you wanted, and I worked side jobs to take care of you, remember? I know that at…at the end, we had a little fight, but! Even so, we share a profound connection forged through day after day of living and sleeping under the same roof, ri—? Ow! Ow, stop that! I said stop that! At least let me finish!"

Megumin had flung a stone at the immobilized Serena, interrupting her. It hit her in the forehead, and a bruise appeared on Megumin's brow in exactly the same place. She might have been reduced to Level 1, but I guess the revenge curse was alive and well.

I didn't know what had Megumin so worked up, but she was getting ready to throw another rock; Darkness attempted to hold her back, while I cast Heal on her to try to calm her down. It must have felt nice, because she smiled; meanwhile, Serena, watching us, seemed to think of something. "Y-yeah, that's it! If you kill me, Lady Regina's power will kill you, too! I'm not bluffing; you saw it work just now! If you see what I'm saying, then let me go this instant! If I fall from this height, I'll die for sure! All of you who strung me up, know this: You'll all perish as well!"

She looked triumphant, but the Axis followers didn't so much as bat an eyelash. They simply said, """"So what?""""

The unfathomable response left not just Serena but the three of us, too, lost for words.

One of the female believers smiled at Serena, who still looked uncomprehending, and said, "You seem to be under some sort of misapprehension. We're Axis believers. Yes, believers in the very Axis Church. And among the things we believe is that when we die, we shall go to be with Lady Aqua. We shall be united with the very goddess we adore! And… And…! After we die, we shall be reincarnated in the world Lady Aqua oversees! We shall be reborn in the paradise called Ja-pan!"

"Huh?"

What did she just say?

Why was she talking about Japan?

Serena looked at the woman, dumbfounded. Zesta spoke as if on behalf of all the believers. "Ja-pan. Lady Aqua tells us that land is like a paradise. People such as myself, whose interests span *well* beyond two genders, can live unashamed there… And not only that! I hear it's over-flowing with books that cater to every possible taste, proclivity, and disposition! Yes, we, who are treated as heretics and perverts here, will be able to hold our heads high in that world!"

Please stop.

"Th-they say that a man such as myself—who loves to wear dresses and the like—is actually in demand over there! I would be treated like a queen…!"

Please, please stop.

"In that world, there is no starvation, and everyone is safe; we need fear no monsters. What's more…! They say that books featuring dandy old dudes locked in wrestling matches together constitute their own genre…! And, *and*…! They even sell the forbidden *shota* books! Oh, I…! I'm so grateful that I'm an Axis follower! I'm so glad to be alive…!" a young woman said, her face flushed and her eyes full of tears.

All right, I give up. It's way too late for these people.

Serena, tears still beading in her eyes, could only whisper: "Y-you're fanatics… You're insane…!"

And for once, I had to agree with her.

"Now, then."

Zesta's voice was completely calm; Serena shivered up in the tree.

"Perhaps you'd be so kind as to answer Master Kazuma's questions?" He sounded so collected. Serena looked back and forth between me and him.

"I want to know about the Demon King's army," I said. "How many enemies are left at his castle, and what are their weaknesses? Oh, and fill me in on the king himself, too, of course."

6

"By today, the Demon King's daughter will have already left the castle at the head of the king's forces. In other words, there are no generals defending the castle. But of course, there's a reason for that." Serena spoke as calmly as she could, considering she was still hanging from the tree. "A long time ago, Wiz attacked the castle, right after she became a Lich. She forced her way through the barrier around the castle—just blew it right open with her magic. After that, the longest-serving general retired and took over the job of guarding the castle gate."

"Sounds like someone who must be pretty damn strong. Who are they, and how do they fight? And what's their weakness?" I asked.

Serena, who had become awfully forthcoming, said, "'Pretty damn strong' is right. This person has established a magic circle within the

Demon King's castle that draws power directly from the demon realm. The catch is that they can't leave the magic circle. But while they're in it, they wield immense power. The constant flow of magical energy means every wound inflicted heals immediately, and the guardian is surrounded by a powerful barrier of their own so that normal attacks can't touch them. They're a powerful wizard in their own right, after all. If you try to come at the castle head-on, they'll smash you with magical attacks powered by an endless stream of magical energy, and that'll be it for you."

Ugh, this guardian didn't sound like any fun...

"So how do we take them down? Any way to just slip past them?"

Serena somehow managed to shrug despite being tied up; it was kind of impressive. "You can't take them down. You can't get through their personal barrier without serious firepower, and even if you did manage to injure them, you'd never be able to keep up with their healing abilities. Even if the castle wasn't surrounded by a magical barrier, this guardian is like...maybe if all the members of the Crimson Magic Clan attacked at once, relentlessly, they *might* manage something. As for getting past... I don't know. I guess a small unit might be able to sneak in, but the kind of magic you'd need to get through the barrier would call attention to you. Either way, the guardian finds you and blows you away." Her attitude seemed to be that it was pretty hopeless.

So getting through the barrier would call attention to us. But what if Aqua opened a hole in the barrier?

"I guess you could say this guardian is more dangerous than the Demon King himself, in a way," Serena said. "As far as I know, he's the most powerful wizard in the entire world."

That got a shiver out of Megumin.

So as long as this guy was in that magic circle, they were more powerful than Wiz? Well, I'd think of how to deal with it on the way. Right now, I had something else to worry about...

"Okay, now the important part. The Demon King..."

"Uh-uh." Serena seemed set on refusing that particular request.

"You're going to kill me anyway, right? I've told you everything I'm going to tell you. Or, what—want to make a deal like last time? Here's the conditions: You let me get away. You promise that, I'll tell you about the Demon King." And then she smirked again.

"You think you're in a position to negotiate? Use your brain. I've got a whole crowd of religious nutjobs behind me just itching to bash your head in. We have ways of making you talk…"

"I'd like to see you try. Torture doesn't work on me. It bounces right back on whoever inflicts it. Now, if you're going to kill me, then kill me! I'll take that information you want to my grave!" she crowed. A grin appeared on her face, but if you looked closely, you could see that she was trembling ever so slightly. She was putting on a tough act, but she was probably desperate to survive.

I was just trying to decide what to do when Darkness stepped up and said, "Why don't you leave this to me, then?" Her cheeks were flushed, and she was clenching and unclenching her hands in excitement.

N-no way… Is she going to…?

"My indomitable will can't be overcome by a little pain! I'm going to give you the full course now, and the first one of us to make a squeak is the loser! Maybe a little heat would help… N-no, I think first—"

"H-hey, stop that, you pervert! Hey! Why are you taking off my shoes? …Whoa, whoa, whoa! What do you want with my toes? What is that, a brick? Where'd you get that from? Stop, I see the corner of that thing! Just what do you have in mind?!"

Serena was growing ever more frantic as Darkness approached. But at that moment, Zesta, who'd been watching the scene silently, suddenly exclaimed:

"I have received a prophecyyyyy!!"
""""?!"""""

Everyone was startled. Zesta had been so quiet and composed until that moment. Now he was visibly trembling, his eyes wide, as if he'd had the most astonishing insight. What was this prophecy or whatever? I had nothing but bad feelings about it...

"I've realized the most astonishing thing. This must surely be a revelation from Lady Aqua..."

"What's the matter, Lord Zesta?"

"Yes, what revelation have you received?"

A stir swept through the Axis believers, while Zesta looked straight at Serena. "Miss Regina Follower. It seems that when someone does harm to you, that harm rebounds back on them. Is that correct?"

"Huh? Y-yeah...that's...that's right." She spoke very quietly, intimidated by the force of Zesta's gaze.

"One more question, then," he said. "Are you a virgin?"

"You don't mince words, do you?! I may serve a dark deity...but she's still one of the gods. I think you can glean your answer from that," Serena replied, sounding just a little embarrassed.

At that, Zesta grabbed his head in his hands and fell to his knees. "Aaahhhh, what a revelation! In other words, I myself—a man! Were I to defile the purity of this follower of Regina...! At that very moment, I, though a man, could know the sensation of being deflowered! Is this not a miracle akin unto virgin birth?!"

"You're not making any sense! I don't understand what you're saying! And I don't want to!" Serena exclaimed.

I didn't get it, either.

"Lord Zesta, p-please let me! Please afford *me* this opportunity! Then I might taste what it is to truly be a woman!"

"That's no fair! You always keep the best stuff for yourself, Lord Zesta!"

"Naw, let me do it! I'll probably never get another chance at this priceless opportunity as long as I live!"

First the goth-Loli person, then the other believers started clamoring.

"Eek! Stop! St—! Th—they're...they're gonna violate me! Kazuma! Kazumaaa! I was wrong! I'll tell you everything! Just stop them!"

7

"*Power Up*! *Protection*! *Blessing*! Now that Regina follower's chastity is mine! If you think you can defeat me in *this* state, then go ahead and try!"

"You filthy cheat! Lord Zesta, borrowing Lady Aqua's power to use buffs like that is a dirty trick!"

"Traitor! Monster!! Using your Arch-priest position in this way is a clear abuse of power!"

While the Axis followers started a really juvenile fight over Serena, I ignored them and crouched down in front of her where she was trembling helplessly. "All right, Serena. I've got one idea that might save you. Cough up the info about the Demon King. Then maybe I'll help you."

"Y-y-y-you mean it?! You'll really get me out of the clutches of those fanatics? I'm trusting you here. I'm trusting you—do you hear me?!" Still tied up, she looked at me with pleading eyes. She must have been really terrified. I just nodded, and she started spilling the details. "The Demon King… He's old enough that his combat power isn't actually that great. But the special abilities passed down by his tribe…those are powerful. I'd go so far as to say that it's that power that allows him to *be* the Demon King."

"Special powers?" I asked, and Serena nodded.

"Yeah, that's right. The Demon King has powerful abilities, just like you guys with the weird names. Like…just by being around him, monsters and demons power up to the point that even a puny goblin could take on a decent adventuring group all by itself."

"That's broken!"

If even a goblin could get that powerful, how strong must the guards around the Demon King be?

"But that's not all. He can also confer protection on his subordinates. You remember how the Dullahan Beldia had unusually high resistance to holy magic, right?"

What, so he could grant status enhancements that even eliminated a monster's weaknesses? That was just lazy game design.

Serena smiled a little, seeming to guess what I was thinking. "You ought to give up the idea of beating him in a fair fight. If you want to take out the Demon King, a better plan would be to attempt to assassinate him when none of his friends are around. You should know, though, that his daughter inherited most of his abilities. That's why she's leading the bulk of the army in the attack on the capital. As he is now, the Demon King wouldn't be able to extend his powers across the whole of his army. But I doubt he'd have any trouble strengthening a monster in the same room. So as long as he's around, you'd best consider every personal guard he has with him to be as strong as one of his generals."

Well, shit.

I'd thought I might consider taking out the Demon King if it didn't seem like too tall an order, but that whole idea was obviously out the window now. In other words, once we had Aqua back, I would talk to Megumin and the others who were all fired up until they came around; then we could all escape using Yunyun's and my Teleport abilities.

I thought I had an idea of how to persuade Aqua: I could tell her that the Demon King was already getting up there in years, and we could just sit around and enjoy our lives until he kicked the bucket due to natural causes. Yeah, that seemed like the most realistic plan.

Okay, that was what I would do. If I told everyone else what Serena had just told me, they would have to see the sense in it.

"How about that? Happy? I don't know much else about the Demon King. Just that as he's gotten older, his daughter has become the apple of his eye, and that it's made personnel management kind of tricky."

"Oh yeah, you're fine. Anyway, it looks like they're almost done arguing," I said, glancing toward Zesta and the others.

"Ha! Ha! Ha! O great Lady Aqua, look upon me! Watch as I vanquish these evil heretics!"

"You old bastard, treating us like unbelievers!"

"Just 'cause you can use a little magic, you let it go to your head! We have Lady Aqua's blessing, too! Do it! Get him!!"

Zesta, despite being alone and barehanded, was handily beating the rest of the believers into submission. He might have been a pretty crappy excuse for a human being, but the old guy was still Most Important Whatever, and with all his buffs, he looked like he could take on an ogre.

Finally, Zesta wiped at his brow with a towel, like he was working up a sweat at the gym. "How about it? Have you finished your little talk? We'd like you to hand over our heretic now."

"Eek!" Serena trembled; the female believers came and stood near her. Their eyes were even more terrifying than Zesta's. They looked ready to kill her on the spot.

"Kazuma… K-K-K-K-Kazuma…!" Serena looked at me beseechingly, probably hoping for that plan to save her that I'd promised her. In answer to her unspoken plea, I produced a sheet of paper.

The Axis profession of faith that had been in our carriage.

In other words…

"Do you hereby repent of all your former deeds, reject all religious faiths you've embraced to this point, and promise to worship, venerate, and revere the goddess Aqua? How about it? Feel like becoming a devout Axis disciple?" I asked.

Serena, looking like she might burst into tears, whispered: "Y-you can't be serious…"

"C'mon, lackey! Stop sniffling! We haven't got all day!"

"Y-yes, sir! Sorry, senior!"

"Senior, huh? I like the sound of that! Call me senior, too!"

"Eek! Wh-what can I do for you, s-senior…?"

"Now listen here, lackey! Don't let it go to your head just 'cause the boys are soft on you. First things first: Go buy everyone here a Neroid. I'll have a Hellishly Heavenly Sweet-n-Sour Neroid—the one they only sell in summer."

"B-but, senior, it's almost winter…"

"Did you say something?"

"Nothing! I-I'll go get it! I'll try every town in the area until I find it!" Serena gave them a smile, although her eyes were brimming with tears and the corners of her mouth were twitching.

"All's well that ends well," I said.

"How is this *well*?!" Serena snapped. She was going to be carted back to Arcanletia to repent everything she'd done to date and given an appropriate punishment. At the same time, she was going to be the lackey of the Axis Church, made to work like a dog, for as many years as she'd been a sinner.

I just prayed I was the only person she'd ever actually killed.

Everything was pretty much wrapped up, and I was just thinking about returning my focus to the Aqua situation when someone called: "Well, Master Kazuma. Shall we get going?"

"Darkness, squeeze over a little more. You *stick out* in various places and take up a great deal of space. Couldn't you make yourself a bit more compact?"

"I-it's not as if I *like* being this endowed. I think you might be a little *too* compact, Megum— Ouch! Ow, ow, Megumin, stop pulling my hair…!"

As the two of them argued, we heard: "Ha! Ha! Ha! Now, now, small chests and muscly busty types are equally necessary to this world. You mustn't fight; that's the main thing. Although if you truly wish to settle the matter, I will happily referee. Just let me have a look, and I'll deliver the final judgment!"

Zesta had volunteered to be our driver, since the only horses we had were the ones corrupted by the Axis believers.

"Listen, creep, no sexually harassing my friends. That's *my* right and mine alone. I'll kick your old ass outta this moving carriage without thinking twice."

"If this idiocy continues, we'll shove you *both* out of the carriage. Megumin, are you sure it's safe to have this guy with us? He didn't need to be the one to drive the horses, did he? Couldn't one of the other Axis believers have done it?" Darkness kept looking uneasily at Zesta in the driver's seat.

"I'm not sure I know what you mean," Zesta said. "I boast the greatest strength of anyone in the Axis Church. There's no one better to ensure your safety along the way. I *shall* see you safely to Lady Aqua." He grinned, ignoring the dirty look Megumin gave him at the word *greatest*.

Incidentally, we were in one of those two-passenger carriages. I had begged for a passenger seat, but they'd turned me down, and I ended up squeezing into the driver's bench with Zesta.

"Ah, the warmth of a young man. What a beautiful reward! Lady Aqua, you have my thanks!"

"I wish you would shut up. Hey, Megumin, Darkness. You *sure* you don't want to trade places?"

"I—I certainly do not; I'm almost positive I would be sexually harassed."

"Y-yeah, same. I'm used to being harassed by you, Kazuma, but with that guy, it's a little..."

No dice, huh?

"If you're ready, then. Shall we be off? My dear fellows, I leave the rest in your hands!"

One of the female believers smiled. "Yes, sir. And we pray that you will be of assistance to Lady Aqua on our behalf, Lord Zesta."

"'Kay, see ya, Serena. I think it'll be easiest if you just give up and go full Axis believer as soon as you can."

"Shaddup and get lost, ya jinx!" Serena's trembling voice was the last thing I heard behind me as Zesta cracked the reins and we set off for the Demon King's castle...!

"I'm amazed to see you here, Lady Aqua. I never imagined we were in the same caravan!"

A guy with a magic sword had driven off the crabs and the ogres. I wasn't sure what he was talking about, but who could blame me? It was all so sudden.

"Yeah, it's been a long time, Magic Sword Guy. Wow, fancy meeting you in a place like this…"

"Yunyun! Oh, Yunyun! Thank you for saving me, Yunyun! Now you *have* to let your Big Sis give you a hug of gratitude!"

"You haven't changed a bit, Cecily!"

While I was having my reunion with Magic Sword Guy, Cecily was embracing Yunyun.

"To think, Lady Aqua, when you were most in need, we just happened to be in the exact same place. This must be fate, or a miracle, or…"

"Yunyun, let's eat some crab! Thanks to Lady Aqua, we've got a big haul of Blue Crabs! We can all have a crab party tonight!"

"Stop that, Cecily. Mr. Mitsurugi is trying to be serious… Did you say a party? A crab party…all together…"

Magic Sword Guy frowned a bit at the way Yunyun kept muttering "together, together." "N-no, we can't have a party here, okay? Besides, I took out those ogres, and ogres have a strong sense of loyalty to their comrades. I'm sure they'll come around trying to find out what happened to the others. Remember, we're here to help Lady Aqua on her journey to defeat the Demon King. Now that we've found her, we need to make for the king's castle as fast as we can…"

"Y-yeah, that's right! I guess… I guess this is no time for a crab party…" Outwardly, Yunyun agreed with Magic Sword Guy, but you couldn't miss the way her shoulders slumped.

"No crab party? Well, I never! Lady Aqua provided these crabs for us! I don't care how hunky you are, big guy—I won't accept this!"

"I'm sorry, you're…Miss Cecily from Arcanletia, right? I think we met at the church there."

I guess Cecily and Magic Sword Guy knew each other.

"Goodness, we've met before?" Cecily said. "Oh, that's right—you're the magic sword guy who came to the Arcanletia church and tried to pick me up by saying you wanted a priest!"

"I wasn't trying to pick you up! Anyway, I would have been happy with any Axis priest. I never said anything about you specifically!" Then, though, Magic Sword Guy seemed to snap out of it. "Lady Aqua, I let myself get distracted there, but please allow me to be clear. We came after you in order to aid you on your quest to rid this world of the Demon King. Long ago, the foremost fortune-teller of the Crimson Magic Clan read my fortune, and this is what she said: *'You will meet an Axis priest, a pivotal person who might well influence the destiny of this world.'* She went on to say, *'Whatever happens, you must protect this person.'* I realize now! She must have been speaking of—"

"Lady Aqua! A hunky younger guy is proposing to me!"

"I'm not talking about you, Cecily! Oh, Lady Aqua, wait! It's extremely important that we talk about—"

Magic Sword Guy and Cecily seemed busy, so I decided to enjoy some crabs.

*   *   *

We ended up spending the whole night enjoying our crab party.

"Lady Aqua, Lady Aqua. There's something the unworthy Cecily wishes to confess." Sitting in the Arcanletia-bound carriage, Cecily was looking at me seriously.

"Why so concerned all of a sudden, Cecily? I don't know what you did, but you know I'm happy to forgive most any sin you commit, right? I can come apologize with you if you need me to."

"Is that true, Lady Aqua? I've done *so many*— Ah, ahem. No, that's not what this is about." She looked like she could hardly bring herself to speak. "Lady Aqua. I, Cecily, attempted to delay you as much as possible in meeting up with Megumin and the others, but it seems I've done all I can do. I brought along all kinds of games to distract you, milady, but it seems we'll arrive in Arcanletia within the hour."

"I'm sort of bothered that you would attempt to do that, but knowing you, I'm sure you thought it was for the best. First that ghost girl, now you… I wonder why everyone keeps trying to slow me down. But it's all right; I forgive you."

Cecily smiled at that and said, "Out of all the adventurers I've known, I would say that your party might have the strongest chance of actually defeating the Demon King. But you know, as for me personally…" She stopped before she could say anything more. "It would be inappropriate for me to speak further. From this point on, a low-level priest like myself could only be a burden. I beg you to stop by the Axis church when we get to Arcanletia. And make the following request of Lord Zesta and the others…" Then Cecily whispered something in my ear. Finally, she concluded, "Unworthy as I am, I pray for your safety and success! Let me give you the best parting gift a poor excuse for a priest like me can manage… May Lady Aqua's blessing go with you! *Blessing!*"

Smiling broadly, she pronounced a magical blessing on all of us.

Chapter 5

A Full Stop for This Journey!

1

We left Serena behind and rode down the narrow path with Zesta at the reins. So far, things were going pretty smoothly. Without a certain someone to cause trouble, everything was going great. Except...

"Hey, Gramps. It's great that you're driving us and everything, but you've been breathing pretty heavily for a while now, and it's beyond uncomfortable."

Yeah. Everything except the relentless panting from beside me.

"Fret not. It's merely a biological phenomenon."

"My ass! It never stops with you, does it? Hang on... What's that?" I was drawing away from Zesta, wondering what I would do about the old fart, when I noticed a dark shadow ahead of the carriage. It was still a ways off, but when I used my Second Sight skill to get a good look at it...

"Ugh, it's a manticore. Let's take a detour, Gramps. I know there was a side street on the way here. Let's go around that way."

Ahead of us stood a manticore, a creature that had left me with substantial trauma once. It was a powerful beast with a poison stinger in its tail, and it would try to stab you in the butt with it. This monster, which you might call a natural enemy of mine, gazed at us from a distance. Was it already too late to run away...?

I was desperately trying to think of a way out of this, but Zesta said, "No, we'll go straight ahead."

"Are you nuts? That thing is the worst kind of bad news. I don't know how strong you are, Gramps, but…"

Zesta didn't so much as slow down. In fact, he picked up speed, clattering straight toward the manticore. "Now, you shall witness the power of an Axis disciple. A manticore is hardly worth a second glance."

Okay, he talked a big game, but…

"Huh? Look, do you understand the most dangerous thing about a manticore? It's gonna try to stab you with that stinger. One of those things almost *made me an adult.*"

For some reason, Zesta's eyes started to shine like a child's. "Ah, divine consummation! Surely this is the will of the gods!"

"Excuse me, what? Darkness is the only pervert we need around here."

"J-just a second, Kazuma… Something about the way you said that makes me feel…a certain type of way." Darkness must have had some sense that she was a pervert, because she was looking at Zesta with a conflicted expression, and her voice wouldn't rise above a mumble.

"It's all right, Kazuma. This man's humanity may be one matter, but his abilities as an Arch-priest are unquestionable. I can vouch for them."

"Really…? Well, if you say so, I guess I'll trust him…"

As we got close enough that we could make out the manticore without any special skills, the monster's eyes met Zesta's for just an instant.

"……*Gulp.*"

"?!"

When the manticore saw how Zesta swallowed heavily as their eyes met, it got a look of severe distress on its face and flew off.

"Oh! It ran away!" Zesta exclaimed.

"What the hell?! Why would a manticore flee?!"

Zesta watched the monster go with a look of grief. "The Axis Church permits *any* kind of love, so long as it's not with a demon or an undead. As the most important person in the Axis Church, I am an evangelist of love. I give love to all equally, including even magical creatures. Of late, though, they all seem to run away the moment our eyes meet…"

"They *always* run away?! Just how hated are you? Nothing's off the table for you, huh, Gramps?!"

Even the Demon King avoided Axis believers. Now I thought I knew why.

While I was busy being shocked, I heard what sounded like a very out-of-place conversation behind me.

"Look, Darkness, there are Blue Crabs over there engaging in mating activity. I believe the way they grab each other with their pincers is an expression of affection."

"G-gosh, really? But, um, Megumin, why bring that up now?"

I looked back to find Megumin gazing out the window, a distant look in her eyes. "Hey, you can't throw me off that easily! You said you vouched for this old fart! Go back to Arcanletia and get us someone different right now!"

"I said I vouched for his abilities *as an Arch-priest*; I specifically disavowed any comment on his humanity! And I would be just as happy for a replacement as you, if I thought we could get one!"

"If both of you feel you must continue to argue, then I have an idea. It would be a simple matter for me to stay the mouths of a young man and woman with my own lips."

Zesta's threat got us to shut up immediately.

He actually looked a little deflated and mumbled, "As an Axis disciple, I hope and pray constantly…that one day, peace may come to this world…and then every distinction, including between tribes and even between men and women, might disappear…"

"Yeah, that sounds great. I might even agree…if it wasn't *you* saying it!"

Were *all* Axis believers like this?! When we caught up with their leader, I was gonna give her a piece of my mind!

2

It had been a while since we'd left Arcanletia.

*   *   *

"Wonderful support magic, Lady Aqua. I knew I could expect the best from you. Thank you."

With my buffs, Magic Sword Guy had easily chopped up that manticore. And while I was sure my help had played its part, it was mostly thanks to this guy's magic sword. It was really something, being able to take on an advanced monster like a manticore. If Kazuma had been here, he probably would have run away screaming from the ogres, then come up with some dirty little trick before he came crying to me for help.

"But of course. Anyone injured?" I asked, just to be sure, but it didn't even take a quick look around to know that everyone was fine. The battles always ended in the blink of an eye, too quick for anyone to get hurt.

"We're quite all right, Lady Aqua. It must be thanks to your blessings that we're all safe again. Although I deeply appreciate your concern." Magic Sword Guy smiled broadly, sounding overjoyed. He really *was* hunky. Unlike a certain someone who was in the habit of sleeping till noon (so he always woke up with bed head) and whose soul was so twisted, it even showed in his eyes.

"Great work, Kyouya! With an Arch-priest and an Arch-wizard, life is easy, huh?"

"Yeah, for sure. We didn't even have to do anything."

The spear-wielding girl and the Thief girl were busy lavishing praise on Magic Sword Guy. He gave them each a pat on the head as if to say thanks, and they blushed.

I remembered Kazuma giving Darkness a pat on the head and a smile completely out of the blue once. She'd gotten angry that he'd messed up her hair, and *he'd* gotten depressed that she didn't understand what he was doing. I wished I could let him know that we had a real master of the Pat-and-Smile here. Being able to get a blush out of a young lady just by giving her a pat on the head was a special skill reserved for hunks.

"With this party, we need not fear even the Demon King. Let's go, Lady Aqua! And bring peace back to this world!"

"Oh yeah, sure," I said, just for the sake of saying something to the grinning Magic Sword Guy.

That was when Yunyun came up to me. "Listen to this, Aqua! Wiz in Axel sent word that Kazuma is on his way to come get us right now!"

"Hoh." So apparently all that murmuring Yunyun had been doing *hadn't* been just her talking to an invisible friend.

Still, though, that Kazuma, he never changed. I left him a note specifically so he wouldn't have to worry about me, and he still came after me. That guy! I understood his desire to lean on an older-sister type such as myself, but I needed him to learn to stand on his own two feet eventually.

"You look happy somehow, Aqua."

"Oh, not especially. So? Is it just Kazuma coming after us?"

"No, it sounds like Darkness and Megumin are with him. Um, when I left town, the other adventurers were all worried about you, too, did you know that? They said that when they saw you again, they were going to lecture you until you broke down in tears. Megumin was especially upset."

"Is that right...?"

An upset Megumin put me on my guard. I hoped she was angry because she had more of a heart for her companions than any of them, but I couldn't be sure. Once, when I'd teased her that using the bath after me would bestow a blessing that would make her just as voluptuous as the goddess of water, she'd stayed in the tub so long, she got dizzy. Maybe she was still holding that against me.

I wondered if she would forgive me if I gave her the weird-shaped rock I'd found on this trip and offered a tearful apology.

The monsters kept getting more and more powerful; we could bathe only when we happened to arrive at a town or village; and at night we were mobbed by undead. Honestly, I was starting to feel just the tiniest bit homesick.

Oh, who was I kidding? I regretted ever coming on this journey. I'd gone this far because I'd wanted to look good for Cecily, but maybe it would be okay to turn around now.

"You know, I'm worried that poor, weak Kazuma might get himself

eaten by a frog on the way here. He's so fragile, you'd think he was playing *Spelunker* sometimes. And now at just Level 1, and with those two in tow, I can't imagine how he would make it here safely." That's why I thought it would be best if we fell back for the time being and…

"He'll be okay! I hear Wiz and Vanir took him into a dungeon and helped him level up! He learned all sorts of skills and awakened or something! Um… By the way, what's *Spelunker*?"

…………

"Gosh, what's that about? I never heard any of that! Kazuma said he awakened?! And what's this about him learning all sorts of skills? I somehow have a bad feeling that he's taking my job! Kazuma is not the type to have something as cool as an awakening happen to him! He's Kazuma! He's supposed to struggle against shrimpy monsters and then use dirty, underhanded tricks to defeat big, powerful enemies! How could something so interesting happen to him while I wasn't even there?!"

I took Yunyun by the shoulders and shook vigorously, sending her head flopping back and forth. "I-I-I'm afraid! I d-d-d-don't know! Aqua, please stop shaking me! I left to come after you before Kazuma did his training, so I don't have any details! Magical long-distance communication has many limits…! I only know that Axel's adventurers got together to train Kazuma up and teach him their skills. So about this *Spelunker*…"

I let go of Yunyun's shoulders and started thinking hard. Our shrimpy little Kazuma, awakened? I could just picture his eyes sparkling as he said the word: I knew he and Megumin were cut from the same cloth.

While I stood with my arms crossed, Yunyun kept muttering forlornly about *Spelunker*. I didn't know why she was so hung up on that.

But hey—while I had been out here on a serious quest to take down the Demon King, everyone back in town had been enjoying a fun event like that? Wow, I felt so left out.

After a few minutes of fretting…

…I decided to give up on defeating the Demon King.

*　　　*　　　*

"How about we go home?"

"What are you saying, Lady Aqua?! It was you who said that this was our best chance! This very moment, with the Demon King's forces split between the capital and Axel, leaving no one to guard the castle! It's okay—trust me! We can and will take down the Demon King! I mean, are you really that worried about *him*?!"

Magic Sword Guy was incensed. And I admit, I was a little intimidated by the way he rushed toward me.

Yunyun, though, quickly put herself between Magic Sword Guy and me. "Calm down, please, Mr. Mitsurugi. Are you sure we couldn't wait for Kazuma and the others to catch up with us before going on to the Demon King's castle? It would give us more fighting power when we did make the assault, and it would keep Aqua safer."

Ah, the Crimson Magic Clan, so smart. Always so smart.

I peeked out from behind Yunyun, nodding vigorously to show what a good idea I thought this was. Magic Sword Guy looked a little sad, then spun around, putting his back to us. "We should hurry onward. I know you're worried about that man, Lady Aqua, but the fate of the world hangs on what we do next. Remember, I beg you, why we're on this journey. Have we not come to finish the fight with the Demon King and save those who are weak and suffering in this world, at the very moment when his castle is least defended? It's all right. I'll be by your side, always..."

Gosh, he sounded like the main character in some manga.

What should I do? He was obviously a lot keener on this than I was. When had I decided to save all the world's weak and suffering? Okay, so I might have said something like that to Cecily, but I didn't recall actually starting on this quest because of anything like that...

Magic Sword Guy's two girlfriends looked at me with conflicted expressions. Was he one of those dense pretty-boy types or something? He was *definitely* one of the oblivious types. I'd seen him pat those girls on the head. Come to think of it, he'd said something to Yunyun about just calling him "Kyouya." Magic Sword Guy was obviously trying to get a harem going. Yunyun, though, always flinched back or froze up every time Magic Sword Guy talked to her and insisted on calling him "Mr. Mitsurugi." It wouldn't be easy to add her to his harem.

Still facing away from us, Magic Sword Guy continued. "Whatever happens, I shall protect you. I shall be the armor on which you can most rely, Lady Aqua. I shall be your sharpest blade, cutting down every enemy in our path. Therefore I implore you, don't look to *that* man but lean on me…"

He still sounded like he thought he was the main character, and he was obviously enjoying himself, so I didn't want to interrupt him. But there was one thing I definitely wished I could correct.

The one I rely on most is Darkness.

Several more days passed.

"Are you feeling unwell, Aqua? Ever since we left Arcanletia, you've been sort of…"

Yunyun was talking to me as I stared into space, perched on the luggage rack of the swaying carriage. Incidentally, I guess this carriage belonged to Magic Sword Guy. Figures a cheater like him would have tons of money.

"How could I not be feeling well? Everything's…you know…going really smoothly. In the past, when I've traveled with Kazuma and everyone else, our trips were always more…dramatic. Like, we survived every day by the skin of our teeth. I'm not saying that was a good thing, but this is just kind of…"

…boring.

Yeah, that was it. It was boring somehow.

Usually, Darkness would go charging into a horde of monsters, who would turn her into a punching bag, then Kazuma, on the verge of tears, would go to rescue her, before Megumin blew them all up with an explosion and I, noble as ever, used my healing magic to help the wounded with all due elegance.

Obviously, it was easier when a trip went according to plan, and that was nice. When we did encounter monsters, Magic Sword Guy usually took them down almost as soon as they showed up, and anything he couldn't deal with instantly, Yunyun finished off with her magic. Even Magic Sword Guy's two little friends looked bored without anything to do.

At that moment, though, I just went quiet. I could hardly tell Yunyun that it was all boring.

"Oh, by the way, what did you do when you stopped over in Arcanletia?" she asked. "Cecily said you went to the Axis church there..."

"Oh, that? Oh, *that*!"

Things just kept going smoothly after that.

We went through a series of small villages that served as frontline bases against the Demon King's forces. That led us to take a break in a tavern in one village that was practically a fortress, somewhere awfully close to the Demon King's castle...

"Hey, why aren't they here? It's been *days* since I set out on my journey, but Kazuma hasn't caught up with me."

"Th-that's true... Things have been going so smoothly for us, they probably haven't been able to catch up... Mr. Mitsurugi, are you sure we shouldn't wait even a little while for them?"

"We can't. While we're here, the Demon King's invasion plans must be proceeding apace. In fact, I wouldn't be surprised if the attack on Axel has already begun. I expect many casualties among the townspeople. We need to make sure there are no more victims in the future, and that means getting rid of the Demon King as soon as possible. Besides, that guy's a piece of human garbage who's already given up on going after you once, Lady Aqua. I keep telling you to let me handle the Demon King...!" Magic Sword Guy clenched his fist dramatically. We were on such different wavelengths at this point that I wasn't even sure how to respond. This guy had completely bought into the being-a-fantasy-world-hero thing.

I couldn't help wondering, though: Did Magic Sword Guy really hate Kazuma that much? Granted, he refused to work even when he needed money, had a terrible reputation around town, would gladly hit a woman, would get back at anyone who did anything to him, was so horny and yet so inept with women, so weak and yet willing to talk tough, immediately bowed down to anyone with a little authority, but also never hesitated to try to use his powerful connections...

"Hey, Yunyun, I'm stuck! I was going to try to stick up for Kazuma, but surprisingly, all I can think of are his bad qualities!"

"A-Aqua, you can't say that out loud. Kazuma would cry if he heard you!"

Magic Sword Guy smiled thinly and got up from his seat. "You just rest here, Lady Aqua. I'm going to go talk to the villagers and try to find out more information about the way to the Demon King's castle." Then he left the bar. The two girls, who had been sitting at the table with us, scrambled after him.

....

"I know he's got a lot of bad qualities, but...he's got a few good ones, too. Like how even though everyone always causes problems for him and makes his life hard, in the end he always goes, *Guess I've got no choice*, and sorts things out. Somehow, Kazuma's always the one we end up counting on."

"I w-wish you'd have come up with that sooner," Yunyun said.

This is so boring.

Our trip was going off without a hitch, with no trouble to speak of. Sure, there had been small problems in some of the villages along the way, but...really small ones. It's true. Even when I put a cup of water on my head as if I was about to do one of my party tricks...

"A-Aqua, everyone's staring at you! A woman shouldn't make herself look so ridiculous!"

...Yunyun was the only one there to make a quip at me. When I'd done this in front of Magic Sword Guy, he'd just watched me with a smile and hadn't said anything. A certain short-tempered someone would have come up with a cutting remark every time I did anything.

With the eyes of the entire bar on me, I flicked a little seed with my thumb, sending it flying into the cup on my head...

*　　*　　*

I was putting the bar behind me. Yunyun rushed to keep up. "A-Aqua, what are we supposed to do with all these tips? Are you sure about this? Everyone was so excited, and you're just going to walk away?"

"It's all right. Anyway, I don't need tips. I'm not a performer; I can't accept those. I wonder if there's an Axis church around here. We could donate them…"

As I was looking for a church, I spotted a crowd. It looked like the villagers were gathering around a reservoir. "I wonder what's going on over there," Yunyun said. "It doesn't look very good."

"Maybe we should go see. If they're having trouble with the water supply, I might just have a chance to shine."

I started to head over, but Yunyun stopped me in a panic. "W-wait! I'll go first and ask them what's happening! I mean, Aqua, you always seem to get caught up in the worst things, and I'm sure this is another one…"

Yunyun really was the worrying type. Yet, somehow, at that moment, she looked just like Kazuma when he was begging me not to do anything silly. The whole idea left me wanting to, well, do something. At least…a little something.

"Just who do you think I am? It'll be fine, Yunyun. When you have water trouble, you call the Axis Church! And as an Axis Arch-priest, this problem is as good as solved!"

"Aqua, I already have a terrible feeling about this! Ohhh, wait!"

I strode over to the crowd of people and said, "Are you having some kind of problem with your water? I happen to be a passing Axis Arch-priest. You know what they say: When it comes to water, think of the Axis Church! Yes, you can count on the Axis Church!"

"Th-the Axis Church!"

"Hey, is that one of those Axis believers? Better keep your distance…"

The people of the crowd greeted me with looks of awe. I wondered, though, why there were a few looks of terror among them as well.

Finally, after a lot of nudging one another with their elbows, one man stepped forward and said to me, "Ahem, as a matter of fact, the village's reservoir is... Well, you can see it. The pond has become polluted, and some young Brutal Alligators have moved in. Those monsters produce a potent poison when defeated, so we can't just go killing them. They hate clean water, so if you were to purify the reservoir, they would probably move out..."

"I see. Yes, you've got it really rough. Well, I guess I'll be on my way."

Yunyun grabbed my arm before I could slip away. "Aqua, where are you going?! What happened to all that confidence?!"

"Yunyun, let go of me! I have bad memories of those gators! You were right after all! I'm starting to share your feeling that this won't go well...!"

"O-okay, okay, just don't run so fast, you'll tri— Oh!"

""""""Oh!"""""""

When Yunyun let go of me, I immediately went tumbling right into the reservoir.

"Aqua, I'm so sorry! I'll pull you out, just— Ahhh! The Brutal Alligators are coming right for you! Hold on—this is an emergency, so I'll prioritize eliminating the monsters!"

"P-please don't do that! We'd be grateful to be rid of them, but what will happen to our precious water supply? We'll be done for!"

"H-he's right! Everyone, put your heads together! Let's think of something! I've got it! Bring a pole of some kind! We'll pull that young lady out of there!"

While the crowd held Yunyun back, the alligators were making a beeline for me in the water...

"I wish you'd skip the committee and either pull me out or get rid of these things! Why do alligators like me so much anyway?!"

The water in the surprisingly deep reservoir came up to my chest, and the alligators were closing in fast.

When I looked, though, I saw the water around me becoming pure. And these alligators were supposed to hate clean water. In other words, they must have seen me with my water-purification abilities and known I was an enemy...!

Faced with the oncoming gators, I cried out to a NEET who couldn't possibly have been there.

"Waaaaaahhh! It's all my fault for leaving home! I'm sorry! Just saa-aave me, Kazumaaaaa!"

3

Everything was going smoothly. So smoothly, I found myself wondering how we'd ever run into so many problems in the past. Sure, having Zesta there as a monster repellent was part of it, but I think an even bigger part was the absence of a certain walking troublemaker.

In every little village we stopped in, Zesta wanted to join me in the bath or sleep in the same room as me, but other than the little bouts of sexual harassment he aimed at the three of us, our trip was essentially problem-free.

Along the way, we encountered a harpy, a werewolf, and even a lamia and a centaur. I finally got used to the madness that gripped Zesta each time we encountered one of these creatures; he'd go chasing after them, and they would run away. Just about the time I was starting to wonder whether the Axis Church was the *true* enemy we should be seeking to destroy, we arrived at a certain small village.

Maybe it doubled as a frontline outpost against the Demon King's army, because it was laid out like a fortress. The inhabitants were all armed, and that special charge in the air that you only find on the front lines was…

"I am curious about this village. It seems rather cozy. And I don't sense a hint of nervousness, do you?"

…that special charge was nowhere to be found.

"Yeah, I wonder what's up. You'd think they could afford to be a little more cautious. A village this small, it could get attacked anytime."

That was when we heard someone laughing, along with a conversation that seemed designed to answer our question.

"My goodness, that priest was something else! Almost like a goddess!"

"That's so true! Who would have imagined that she could purify our only water source just by throwing herself into it?! You don't see many people like her these days—people who have really got it together!"

....

"Um, excuse me, could you tell me more about what you were just talking about?" I asked the two of them, trying to act nonchalant. They looked suspicious for a second, but when they saw I was dressed like an adventurer, they relaxed.

"Thing is, the village's reservoir had gotten so polluted that some Brutal Alligators had moved in. But a *very* beautiful priest happened by, and she flung herself in front of the awful creatures to purify the water."

A very beautiful priest who nearly sacrificed herself...?

"Oh. Must have been someone else."

"I agree. We do not know any priests as impressive as that."

"Mm, definitely not. No question."

"I-if you insist on bad-mouthing our deity, you'll incur divine wrath, you know," Zesta interjected, sweating at the way we were all so sure it wasn't her.

That was when the other guy said, "She was an Axis priest with blue hair. The way she threw herself into the reservoir, it was almost like she'd stumbled and fallen, and her voice, it was almost like she was screaming, but the water was purified as we watched..."

"That's definitely Aqua. She fell in."

"It is certainly Aqua."

"Yeah, that's Aqua. No question."

"You're all— No, you know what? I won't say anything more..." Zesta was giving us a rather strange look while I tried to ascertain the whereabouts of the idiot who had fallen in the pond.

"Oh, the priest? She's... Well, we warned her it was dangerous and told her not to go, but she and some friends set off for the Demon King's castle. That was several hours ago now."

""""Several hours...?!""""

We'd caught her!

Wait...several hours?

We'd *almost* caught her! Just a little farther!

I could barely hide the joy welling up within me...

"H-hey, what? What are you two grinning at?"

"Nothing. You just looked very happy. Lately, there's been no end to your quips, bad attitude, and annoyance, and I simply wondered if things might at last go back to normal."

"Oh-ho, better back off, Megumin. You know he can never admit how he feels. You might just make him turn all prickly again."

For a brief second, I considered stealing their panties right then and there and giving them to Zesta to thank him for bringing us this far, but I didn't have the time to waste.

"Okay, when we get back to Axel, Megumin, you're forbidden from using Explosion for three days; I'm going to use Drain Touch on you constantly to keep you from doing it. And, Darkness, I'm going to occasionally change the oil you use to polish your armor for tempura oil. All right, let's get going, and fast!"

"K-K-K-Kazuma?! You're joking, right? You don't have to go quite *that* far, do you?!"

"Y-yeah, yeah! That joke isn't funny... It *is* a joke, isn't it, Kazuma? S-say it's a joke, please! This armor means so much to me that I've even put my name on it. Y-you wouldn't *really* do it, would you?"

4

Zesta cracked the whip, and the carriage set off at a breakneck pace. The Demon King's castle was supposedly less than half a day's ride from the village.

I was sort of surprised a village so close to the castle had managed not to get itself destroyed, but apparently there were a few reasons for that. For one, the Demon King's lackeys didn't eat food; they fed on spiritual energy and vibes. And the village doubled as a source of sustenance for them. They never sucked out enough spiritual energy to kill anyone, so the villagers quietly went along with it.

The village had been built in hopes of forging connections with the Demon King's forces. Surprisingly, even within his army, there were those who wanted to talk. A lot like how on Earth, even countries that are at war want to have a diplomatic pipeline to each other for when push really comes to shove.

I'd assumed this place was trapped in a tragic, pay-for-blood-with-blood cycle of violence, but it turned out connections could pop up when they really mattered. Could it be that the Demon King's army wasn't just a bunch of lawless villains?

I didn't know how much time had passed, but while I was busy thinking about the Demon King's army, the carriage started to slow down, and then it came to a halt.

"What's going on?" I asked.

"We have a problem. The horses are terrified. The castle must be close," Zesta replied. I looked at the horses, which had stopped dead and were refusing to go any farther, obviously frightened of something. Well, this was no good. Aqua and the others had probably come by carriage, too, so we weren't going to catch up with them on foot...

Then I felt Megumin tug on my sleeve; she pointed silently.

"Is that their carriage?"

A carriage sat right out there. Maybe the one Mitsurugi and the others had taken or maybe someone else's. In any case, the horses appeared to have been released. If the carriage did belong to Mitsurugi, they'd probably let the horses go, on the assumption that they would all be able to Teleport back home with Yunyun.

"They must be close," I said. "Okay, we'll go on foot, too. If I know Aqua, when she actually sees the castle, she'll be too frightened to do anything and end up just moping around. Thanks for your help, Gramps. This is far enough. You turn around. We'll take it from here."

"Hmm? I daresay having me with you could turn out to be helpful, no? Besides, I'm quite disappointed not to get to join in something as delightful as invading the Demon King's home base."

Well, no question he'd proven himself useful, but…

"If worse comes to worst, the rest of us can get out of here with Teleport. But that spell can only transport up to four people at a time. We might be able to link up with Yunyun, but her party already has five people. Combined with the three of us, that means we can get away in exactly two Teleports. Yunyun and I use our spells at the same time and poof, we're gone. But hey… If you don't mind being left behind in an emergency…"

"I await good tidings of your quest in Arcanletia! I'll be going, then!"

We grinned a little as we got down from the carriage. I grabbed the luggage from the luggage rack and pulled it onto my back; then I made sure everyone was with me before I shook Zesta's hand. "All right, Gramps. Try to cut down on the harassment, mm'kay?"

"But then I would lose eighty percent of my reason for living. In any event, hold on just a moment, everyone." From the driver's seat, Zesta stretched out his hands toward us. "*Power Up! Protection!* And…*Blessing!*"

He cast a series of buffs on us. Strength enhancers and defense boosters. That last Blessing spell was probably just for good measure.

"Very well, everyone, I pray for your success. Or should I say…may Lady Aqua's blessings go with you!" Then he smiled with genuine kindness, the first time I'd seen him look like a real cleric, before he set the horses galloping off again.

Aqua's blessings, huh? That was nice and all, but we were about to go rescue the goddess herself. I waved as the carriage disappeared with the old guy I somehow couldn't bring myself to hate.

"…Huh?! I just checked my luggage, and I'm missing a pair of panties!" Megumin exclaimed.

"What?! Hey, me too!" Darkness cried.

They'd been going through their belongings, looking for anything they could jettison to make their loads even a little bit lighter as we went after Aqua, when they'd made the discoveries.

…Maybe we really should destroy the Axis Church.

*   *   *

Perhaps it was the buffs that made my step feel so light. As I all but pranced down the road after Aqua, loaded with baggage, we ran into a series of monsters.

Already-defeated monsters, that is.

The road wound up a hill that was littered with monster corpses. They looked like they'd each been brought down with a single stroke of a magical sword: Some were missing their heads; others were sliced clean in two. It was kind of gross, actually...

"Hey, Kazuma, this corpse is still fresh. Aqua and the others can't be too far ahead!" Darkness, checking the monsters' bodies, said quietly. At that, Megumin, unable to contain her excitement, picked up her pace, and Darkness broke into a trot behind her.

"Wait up! The... The baggage is so heavy...! Hey, don't leave me behind!"

"I do not understand how this man can fail to be moved by the prospect of an emotional reunion with his friend! Just throw away all that cargo!"

"Throw it away—real nice!"

"Bah, give it to me! I'll carry it! Sheesh, just when I think you're going to show us your cool side, you come up short... H-hey, this *is* heavy! What's in here, training weights?! You're supposed to travel light on a journey like this! What the heck is in this thing?!"

Darkness might have been complaining, but at least she'd taken the load off my shoulders, literally. I knew it was pathetic, but that was where my base stats left me.

Finally, we crested the hill to see...

"I-it's hideous..." The words slipped out of my mouth.

"Y-yeah," Darkness agreed.

Standing before us was a giant pitch-black castle; anyone could tell it belonged to the boss.

"It's so...so...*cool*!" Megumin whispered, clutching her staff with both hands. These Crimson Magic people. It wasn't even worth quipping anymore...

But at that moment, any other thoughts were cut off completely.

There she was. In the distance, just down by the castle, I could see a familiar blue head.

"I—I *found* her!"

"""?!"""

Darkness and Megumin were startled by my shouting. They squinted into the distance, trying to figure out who I'd found, but they didn't have skills that granted them enhanced sight like I did, so they couldn't tell who it was.

Aqua, with Mitsurugi and the others in tow, was approaching the Demon King's castle, then sticking out her hand as if she was looking for something.

"Aquaaaaa! Hey! Heeeey! I know it's you, Aqua! Argh, dammit!" I clicked my tongue, pulled my bow off my back, and with my Deadeye skill, I—

"Wait-wait-wait! Kazuma, what do you think you're doing?!"

"You may intend to fire an arrow to get her attention, but if you miss your aim even a little bit, it'll go clean through her head! I'm aware of how superb your Luck is, Kazuma, but I also know how terrible Aqua's is!"

Grrr... Now that she mentioned it, that did seem like how this scenario would turn out.

While I was dallying, though, Aqua's outstretched hand began to glow.

"Bah! She's getting inside!"

As I watched, Aqua opened a small hole in the barrier and slipped right through. Mitsurugi and the rest followed her. The moment they were inside, the hole sealed itself up.

This was bad. I didn't know if she would be able to hear me through the barrier. If I started running right now, would I even reach her in time?

Anyway, how could the castle not be protected *at all*? If it'd had even one single guard, we could have caught up to them while Mitsurugi was fighting! Were the Demon King and his army that confident in this barrier?

Beside me, Darkness slumped to her knees, defeated. "How could we make it this far and not be in time...?"

Megumin, still clutching her staff, looked like she might cry. "Wh-wh-what shall we do? Should I have let you try your luck with your sniper shot, Kazuma?!"

While they were blathering, Aqua and the others winked out of view. Yunyun must have used her invisibility magic. That was only going to make it even harder to stop them!

Darkness looked up at me, her expression changing to one of panic. "Y-you must have something, right, Kazuma? At moments like this, you've always got some special plan, some twisted idea..."

Hey, who was she calling "twisted"?

"K-Kazuma..." Megumin looked at me, too, clearly worried, asking with her eyes if I really had nothing up my sleeve.

...Well, to be perfectly honest, I hadn't come completely unprepared. But playing this card would take courage. It would mean gambling everything, the whole cushy life I'd built for myself.

When she saw me fretting...

"Ha-ha..."

...Megumin managed to smile through her sadness. No...looking closer, I saw she was trembling, holding back a storm of tears.

"H-hey, what's wrong? Don't give up now. They got into the Demon King's castle, but Aqua's not dead or anything. You can't go getting all weepy right now, you know?"

I tried to sound lighthearted, but Megumin ground her teeth and said, "No... If only I knew advanced magic. If only I was a real member of the Crimson Magic Clan and not just a spare mage... When I think that then, I might have been able to go after Aqua..."

"Wh-what, why? Is there some kind of magic that could bring down that barrier?"

Megumin shook her head dejectedly. "If I knew the spell Light of Saber that so many Crimson Magickers are so fond of, I might be able to cut through that barrier. That spell can cut virtually anything, so long as the caster has enough power. If only I knew it. If only I'd learned any other magic. Normally it's the wizard's *job* to break through barriers like this one. But I had to be stubborn my whole life. I've never once done *anything* befitting a proper wizard."

Suddenly, and without a word, Darkness took Megumin into her arms.

"If Yunyun was here," Megumin went on, "she would have been able to cut you a path with Light of Saber or else use communication magic to call out to Aqua. Some other Crimson Magic Clan member might have been able to cast something that could get Aqua's attention without alerting the other monsters in the castle…"

Darkness placed a hand on Megumin's head. "You're not the only one who's lived to regret her skill set. If only I'd learned how to take the offensive, our adventures might have been easier. Not just this one, but all the quests we've been on. When it comes to making everyone go out of their way, I've been just as bad as you."

I watched them, the moment at once pathetic and touching.

Why was it that they suddenly had to get all cool and dramatic on me? How was I supposed to follow that?

This wasn't the time to be getting all teary-eyed and introspective. If we just let Mitsurugi handle things, he might actually take down the Demon King for us. But then again, he and his party might run into some random shrimpy monster and rush back crying.

Megumin had called herself a failure of a mage. She was probably thinking of the letter from Crimson Magic Village where she'd been referred to as a spare at best. Normally, she probably would have laughed it off with a haughty snort, but doing this entire journey without our usual companion, Aqua, with us must have taken its toll. She acted tough, but deep down, she was still a kid.

...Er, but if she was still a kid, what did that make me, given that I'd been about to...you know...

Sheesh.

She hardly shut up about explosion magic, and now she was regretting it? Darkness, too: She was Darkness! *If only I'd learned how to take the offensive,* huh?

Well, no shit!

If you were a Crusader who could hit the broad side of a barn, our adventures *would've* been a lot easier! But it was that other idiot who really took the cake. As if it wasn't bad enough that she spent every day just doing whatever she wanted, now she had to drag us all the way out here to come get her. And then she waltzed right into the Demon King's castle!

I can't believe them... Every single one of them...!

"Megumin, listen. The barrier around the castle. You can't blow it away with Explosion, can you?"

"It's impossible... Explosion, which simply creates a burst of magical energy, can damage any enemy at all, and I suppose it might be able to put a crack in that barrier. But..." Then she whispered, pain in her voice: *"I just don't have the firepower..."*

She was still deeply dispirited. I said, "What you're saying is, *one* explosion wouldn't do it, right? But maybe a whole bunch of them in a row could break through?"

"I-it's not possible. A barrier of that magnitude repairs itself gradually over time. Even if there was a way to quickly recover my MP after I let off my spell, I presume the barrier would have fixed itself by the time

I was ready to let off the next blast. And anyway, the moment I fired the first explosion, the Demon King's lackeys would come after us..."

"So you could break it down if you could hit it again and again without pausing?" I pressed.

Megumin, a little bit cowed by the forcefulness of my interrogation, nodded. "Y-yes. But the scale of that barrier—one or two explosions wouldn't be enough. Even Aqua was able to create only a small opening. It would take dozens of—"

"Dozens? You think that would do it? If you could let off that many explosions, you think you could break through that barrier?" I continued to push.

"Yes, I could. To bring the barrier down would take less than thirty... No, less than twenty blasts." She nodded again, as if to say that in this, at least, she had confidence.

Well, that was enough for me.

"Wh-what are you thinking, Kazuma? You're going to use Explosion? That's our trump card. Sure, it might startle Aqua and the others into coming out, but I can guarantee it'll bring the Demon King's minions with them," Darkness said, obviously worried. "Besides, using up our most powerful attack here and now—"

"Darkness, hand me my bag," I interrupted and stuck out my hand for the cargo she was holding for me. Knitting her brow fretfully, Darkness nonetheless slung my backpack off her shoulder and passed it to me.

"You know," I said, "I brought Darkness that armor, but I never got you anything, Megumin." I smiled at her as I undid the string of my bag.

"Wha—? I-it's all right; this is hardly the time for a present. Anyway, I am not one of those high-maintenance girls who gets all upset if she doesn't get expensive gifts, okay?" Megumin chuckled.

Darkness exclaimed, "Hey! Megumin, when you put it that way, it makes it sound like *I'm* high-maintenance...!"

"I am certainly not calling you high-maintenance, Darkness, simply because you swore you would treasure that armor for the rest of your life, and you spend every spare moment polishing it with a broad grin on your face. Indeed, I find it adorable." Megumin smirked at Darkness, who turned a little red.

"Now, now, don't fight. I did go ahead and get you a nice, expensive gift. Just take it."

"Oh, r-really? Y-you certainly didn't have to—"

"I see that grin," Darkness interjected. "I think you might be higher-maintenance than you th— Hey, hey! Do you like pulling my hair that much?!"

While the two of them struggled, I poured out the contents of my pack.

"""..............."""

When Darkness and Megumin saw it, they stopped cold.

"Here's your present. It's all yours. Sorry it's a little late," I said coolly. Megumin started to sweat profusely, while Darkness's mouth worked open and closed and she started to shiver.

"Y-y-y-you... Do you understand just how much this is worth?! How did you even *get* so much of it?!" Darkness was a noblewoman; she ought to have known what it was like to have wads of cash, but her voice was scratching, and she was practically screeching.

"You'd better believe I know how much it's worth. It cost most of my fortune. I made a ton of money with Vanir once, remember? Back when I sold all my intellectual property rights to him to repay your debt, Darkness. Well, he told Wiz to use it to get the highest-quality manatite she could find. And to thank him for helping me out in the dungeon, I bought it all off him before we left on this trip."

Darkness put her head in her hands, looking woozy.

"K-K-K-K-Kazuma, this... This is...!" Megumin pointed at the pile on the ground, at a loss for words.

"The highest-quality manatite Wiz could find, like I said. I remember what you told me when you took some of this stuff off Yunyun. You said a manatite crystal shoulders the MP cost for a spell, right? And that even the best stuff couldn't quite cover one of your explosions."

This time, Megumin couldn't even make a sound.

"And I think I remember you saying something else. That a gem like this wasn't even worth a second glance from a great mage like you. Well, manatite this good ought to be worthy even of the greatest mage. And I'm giving it all to you."

There was a clatter as Megumin dropped her staff. Beside her, Darkness put her hand to her forehead and looked up at the sky.

"Have you lost your mind?" Megumin asked, her voice scratching. "I mean, one piece of manatite of this quality could buy a small house. With all these together, you could buy a small castle!"

"I don't care—use it all up. Just take out that barrier," I said.

Megumin picked up her staff with trembling hands. "Really? You're sure? Manatite is a consumable. You know that, right? When I cast my spell, it'll disappear." Her voice didn't sound quite normal.

I said forcefully, "Seriously, do it. It's my treat. Every last piece of it."

Megumin looked like she was turning a bit feverish from imagining what was about to happen. "A-are you really, truly sure? And anyway, when I use Explosion, you *know* enemies are going to come pouring out of that castle." She gulped heavily. "Including the one Serena talked about—that long-serving former general who's more dangerous than the Demon King. The most powerful wizard in the world…"

I stuck out my hand, preventing her from saying anything more. "I don't care who we're up against. With all your experience and practice, I know your explosion can outrange them. Drop it on the castle from all the way out here. Blow away the Demon King, blow away his lackeys, blow away Aqua for casually walking on in there! It's been one hell of a trip, and I've got some stress to work off, myself! This is where you get to show all those Crimson Magic Clan members who thought so little of you just how good you really are! Money? We can earn more. I'm sick of the trouble the Demon King has caused me, I'm sick of the trouble a certain runaway has caused me, and my tiny, miserly heart can't take anymore! And maybe I can't drop an explosion on that castle, but you can! So help me blow off a little steam!"

"H-h-hey, Kazuma, I think I heard a name that doesn't belong on that list of things to blow away! Anyway, you sound awesome, but you're actually asking someone else to do all the work...," Darkness interjected.

"Sh-shut up!" I shot back, turning red. "Wealth is basically a *form* of power! I mean, how often have you used your power as a young noblewoman?!"

"Huh?! Hold on, what does that even mean? I've never misused my privileges...! W-well...a-almost...never..."

With Darkness's voice getting softer and softer, I stood in front of the two girls and declared, "When we get that idiot back, we're gonna do this right! I've got all kinds of skills now. I'm Kazuma, the elite adventurer! When I think back on sleeping in the stables and being chased around by frogs, this sounds downright easy!"

Megumin, taken aback by this transformation, looked at me. A single tear formed in her crimson eye and ran down her cheek.

"Just leave it to me. I'll make good use of your gift. This is a day I shall not forget for the rest of my life. So there's some wizard in there who thinks they can ignore me and call themselves the strongest mage in the world? I'm going to blow them away, here and now!"

Her words were inspiring, and her eyes, the very source of the Crimson Magic's Clan name, shimmered.

That's what made her the keeper of our firepower.

"Go wild, O strongest mage."

Megumin threw her arms around me and gave me the tightest hug I'd ever felt.

Standing on the hill overlooking the Demon King's castle, I heard a familiar incantation.

"Ahhh… Ahhhh… Can you *imagine* how much even one piece of this manatite is worth…?"

"Shut up, you bankrupt noblewoman! I don't want that armor doing its weird thing to you and sending you charging at whatever comes out of that castle, so just keep your distance and watch!"

"Bankrupt noblewoman?! Wh-who's bankrupt?! I keep telling you, my family just sticks to a frugal budget, that's all—we don't squeeze money out of the people, and we're not bankrupt! Anyway, this is just like that time when you 'bought' me—sometimes you do the most ridiculous things with your money! Two nations at war with each other wouldn't use up the financial resources represented by this much manatite!"

"Seriously, shut up. Believe me, I know this is a weird way to use my money! But you're right, it *is* just like when I repaid your debt and got you back! I've never regretted these large expenses!"

"O-oh, really? Y-yeah, I see, that's great…" Darkness, suddenly embarrassed (and also suddenly a lot more polite), took a step back.

Huh? I hadn't been intending to inspire this sort of atmosphere…

"How dare you flirt when I am about to do something that may never be seen again in the world." Megumin, buried up to her waist in a mountain of manatite, looked thrilled but sounded a little annoyed at the awkwardness that Darkness and I were exuding.

There's this thing called Explosion magic. It's outrageously difficult to learn, of course, and that's not even mentioning the tremendous amount of MP that casting it consumes or the fact that it's virtually always overkill, making it notorious as the spell with possibly the worst cost-benefit ratio in the world.

But at the same time, it's also the most powerful offensive magic available to humanity: One good hit from it can deal damage to any adversary, be they god, demon, or even the Demon King.

"With the manatite you've given me, I will show you a display that even the greatest of the great mages would not be able to replicate. You are about to witness the finest accomplishment of my entire life. I hope you will always remember the honor of being present here today."

There was once a girl, an Arch-wizard, who'd always been dismissed as a "joke mage."

She could cast only one spell a day, and no party anywhere wanted her; even her fellow clansfolk considered her a "spare."

"My name is Megumin! Greatest Arch-wizard of Axel and master of Explosion! Bring on the world's 'greatest wizard' or any demon, or dragon, or even the Demon King himself! I'll show you that I can blow them all away!"

A failure of a wizard who'd spent her life being ridiculed and teased as she chased the dream of being the strongest.

*   *   *

"Explooooooooosiiiioooooooonnnnnn!"

That day, she well and truly claimed the title of the world's strongest wizard.

Afterword

Thanks for picking up *Konosuba*, Volume 16! Your author, Natsume Akatsuki, here.

This was a more serious (?) volume with a pretty minor role for Aqua.

In order to chase after a goddess gone alone on a journey to save humanity, our self-absorbed, cowardly main character had to really train himself up for the sake of his precious companion. He also had to summon the courage to commit to destroying the Demon King. (I think that's about accurate anyway.)

The scene with Megumin at the end of this book is something I've wanted to write since I started posting this story on the web. This party is so dysfunctional that frogs remain mortal enemies for them, yet they've battled more and more powerful opponents and now find themselves taking the fight to the Demon King.

This is the story I've had in mind ever since I started writing *Konosuba*. I hope my readers will stick with me just a little longer.

Oh yeah, less than a month to go now until the *Konosuba* movie makes its theatrical premiere! Our dysfunctional party has "made it big" enough in the world to have a theatrical movie. As an author, it's pretty emotional. By all means, I hope you'll go enjoy the adventures of Kazuma and his friends on the big screen.

Around fall, there'll be an anime of *Kemonomichi*, the manga series I scripted about a pro wrestler going berserk in a pet shop in another world. I definitely hope you'll check it out.

As ever, this volume reached your hands thanks to the effort of everyone involved with it, beginning with illustrator Kurone Mishima and including the editorial, design, and copyediting staff and everyone else at Editorial.

And as is becoming a habit, there's just one thing I really have to make sure I say: To everyone who's supported this series and every reader who picked up this book, my deepest thanks!

Natsume Akatsuki

ドキ
DOKI
(BA-DUM)

ドキ
DOKI

・・・・・
・・・

darkness hiding
in Kazuma's closet

2019.8
Kurone Mishima

It's a raid! A money-fueled raid!

Some people shouldn't be given money… And he's one of them…

At last, **the day has come** when I shall be called Demon King Megumin!

You complained once about beating the Demon King with money, Megumin…

I shan't let my past dictate my future!

We'll tie up the Demon King and give him the business! We'll burn his castle to the ground!

Heeey… Aren't you forgetting someone?!

KONOSUBA
GOD'S BLESSING
ON THIS WONDERFUL WORLD! 17

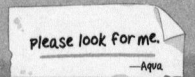

please look for me.
—Aqua